THE ADVENTURES OF
PINOCCHIO
TALE OF A PUPPET

THE ADVENTURES OF

TALE OF A PUPPET

By C. Collodi (Carlo Lorenzini)
Translated from the Italian by M. L. Rosenthal

New translation authorized by the Collodi Foundation

Illustrated by Troy Howell

Lothrop, Lee & Shepard Books   New York

Library of Congress Cataloging in Publication Data

Collodi, Carlo, 1826-1890.
  C. Collodi's The adventures of Pinocchio.

  Translation of: Le Avventure di Pinocchio.
  Summary: Pinocchio, a wooden puppet full of tricks and mischief, with a talent for getting into and out of trouble, wants more than anything else to become a real boy.
  [1. Puppets—Fiction. 2. Fairy tales] I. Howell, Troy, ill. II. Title. III. Title: The adventures of Pinocchio.
PZ8.C7Pi 1983   [Fic]   83-801
ISBN 0-688-02267-7

This translation of
The Adventures of Pinocchio
is dedicated to the memory of
ROLANDO ANZILOTTI
Scholar, friend, and founder of the Collodi Foundation

ACKNOWLEDGMENTS

I am deeply indebted to the late Rolando Anzilotti for the suggestion that I undertake this translation for the centenary celebration of Pinocchio's first appearance in book form in 1883. I am grateful, as well, to Gaetano Prampolini and Laura Coltelli for their careful reading and suggestions—a labor of love growing out of their association with their senior colleague, Professor Anzilotti, at the University of Pisa. They continued both the encouragement and the manuscript-review that he lavished on this book with a devotion matching that of Pinocchio himself during the days just before his human metamorphosis.

Thanks are due, also, for the kind suggestions of Sally M. Gall and David H. Rosenthal.

CONTENTS

THE ADVENTURES OF
PINOCCHIO
TALE OF A PUPPET

CHAPTER

1

O NCE UPON A TIME THERE was—

"A king!" my young readers are shouting.

No, children, you're wrong! Once upon a time there was—*a piece of wood.*

That's all, nothing fancy—a plain little log, just right for a wood stove or a fireplace, to warm up a room in the winter.

Somehow, that log turned up suddenly one day in a poor old carpenter's workshop. His name was Mr. Tony, but everybody called him Mr. Cherry. That's because his nose was so shiny and purply-red, like a very ripe cherry.

When Mr. Cherry saw the log, he began bouncing up and down with excitement. He rubbed his hands together gleefully and gave a great whoop.

"What luck! Just what I needed! Now I can make a nice little table leg for somebody to buy!"

And he picked up his ax to cut the bark off the log and make the wood nice and smooth. But then, with his arm high in the air, he froze in his place. He had heard a tiny, tiny voice whimpering:

"Don't hit me hard!"

What a shock! You can imagine poor Mr. Cherry's surprise. He darted his eyes about the room. Where had the tiny voice come from? He couldn't see anybody. He looked under the workbench. Nobody. He looked into the closet he always kept locked. Nobody. He looked into the big old wastebasket where he put sawdust and wood chips. Nobody. Well! He certainly was worried and puzzled.

"Never mind," he said at last, laughing aloud and scratching his head under his wig. "I'm sure I only imagined that voice. All right, then, I'd better get back to work. I've wasted enough time already."

So he lifted his ax again, and this time he quickly started cutting the bark away from the wood.

"*Ow!* You're hurting me!" It was that same tiny voice.

Mr. Cherry almost fainted. He fell to the floor, so scared that his eyes bulged out of his head, his mouth dropped open, and his tongue flopped down over his chin. He looked like a silly stone face carved on a fountain.

When he could talk again he trembled and stammered with fright.

"But—but—where did that tiny voice that cried '*Ow!*' come from? I looked everywhere in the room but couldn't find a living soul. Can a piece of wood cry out and talk just like a child? I don't believe it! Why, it's nothing but a plain little log, exactly like all the others. I could throw it on the fire and cook my beans with it. But—suppose there really is someone, some tricky rascal, hiding inside it and making fun of me? If there is, I'll teach him a lesson! I've had enough of his teasing!"

And he snatched the poor little log up in both hands and began smashing it against the wall with all his might.

Then he stopped and listened. Was the tiny voice crying

again? He listened for two whole minutes. Nothing.—Five minutes more. Nothing.—Ten minutes more. Still nothing.

"Oh, well, that's that," he said with a sigh. He forced himself to laugh, and straightened his wig to calm his nerves. "I guess I did just imagine the tiny voice crying '*Ow!*' Back to my job!"

Because he was still scared, he began singing to help himself feel a little braver.

He had put the ax aside. Now he started to smooth the wood with his plane. As he moved it back and forth, he heard a giggle, and then—that same tiny voice:

"Hey! You're tickling me!"

And this time poor Mr. Cherry did faint. He toppled over as if he had been struck by lightning. When he woke up he was sprawled on the floor. His face looked completely different. Even his nose, instead of being dark purply-red, had changed to deep blue out of shock and fright.

CHAPTER

2

J UST THEN, SOMEONE KNOCKED.
"Come in," said the carpenter, who was still too weak to get up and open the door himself.

And in popped a lively little old man named Geppetto. The boys of the town used to tease him all the time. They called him Old Corny, because his big yellow wig was just the color of cornmeal mush.

Geppetto had a temper! Better not try calling him Old Corny if you wanted him to like you! He'd fly into a terrible rage, and nothing could be done to stop him.

"Good morning, dear Mr. Tony," said Geppetto. "What are you doing on the floor, my friend?"

"I'm teaching the ants arithmetic."

"Good luck to you, old pal!"

"And what brings you here, my friend Geppetto?"

"My legs! What else? I've come here to ask a favor, good Mr. Tony."

"Ask away. I'm at your service." And the carpenter pulled himself up and knelt in front of Geppetto, pretending to be his slave.

"Well, I had a great idea this morning."

"An idea?"

"I thought I might carve myself a beautiful puppet out of wood, a marvelous puppet that could dance and fence with a sword and do somersaults in the air. I'd take my puppet all around the world and earn plenty of money, enough for bread and wine wherever I go. What do you think of that for an idea?"

"Bravo, Old Corny!" cried the tiny voice that seemed to come from nowhere.

When he heard these words, Geppetto turned red as a chili pepper. He glared at the carpenter and bellowed, "What's the big idea, insulting me?"

"What? Who's insulting you?"

"*You're* insulting me. You just called me Old Corny!"

"Nonsense! I did *not*!"

"Come on! You don't suppose I called *myself* Old Corny? It was you!"

"No."

"Yes."

"No."

"Yes."

They pushed their heads against each other, back and forth, growing angrier and angrier every second. They went from words to fists, and scratched and bit each other, and knocked each other all around the room.

At last they stopped. Mr. Tony found Geppetto's yellow wig held tight in his hand, and Geppetto found the carpenter's grizzled wig clenched between his teeth.

"Give me back my wig!" said Mr. Tony.

"And you give mine back! Let's be friends again."

So these two little old men put their wigs back on their

heads, shook hands, and swore to be buddies forever after.

"Now, my dear friend Geppetto," said the carpenter kindly, "what was it you came here for?"

"A little bit of wood—that's all—to make myself a puppet. Can you help me?"

Mr. Tony suddenly felt happy. He skipped to his bench for the bit of wood that had almost scared him to death and

handed it to Geppetto. But the wood jerked itself out of his hand and whacked poor old Geppetto's bony shins.

"Ouch! Hey, that's a nice way you give your friend a present, Mr. Tony! Do you want to cripple me?"

"*I* didn't do that, I swear!"

"I suppose *I* did it, huh?"

"The wood, the piece of wood—*that's* what did it!"

"Sure, I *know* it was the wood. But you're the one who threw it at my shins!"

"I didn't!"

"Liar!"

"Now you be careful, Geppetto. Don't start insulting me, or I'll have to call you Old Corny."

"Stupid jackass!"

"*Old Corny!*"

"Ugly monkey!"

"*Old Corny!*"

That made three times Geppetto had to hear himself called Old Corny. He went crazy with rage and hurled himself on the carpenter. Nothing could keep them from going at each other all over again, blow for blow, hammer and tongs. *Biff! Bang! Oof! Ouch!*

When the fight was over, Mr. Tony had two more scratches on his dark blue nose, and his dear pal had lost two more buttons from his jacket. So they were even. They shook hands again, and swore to be true buddies for the rest of their lives.

Geppetto picked up his precious bit of wood, thanked Mr. Tony, and limped off home.

CHAPTER

3

GEPPETTO, WHO WAS VERY poor, lived in a tiny basement room. The only light came through a window near the stairway outside his room. His furniture was as plain as could be: an old kitchen chair, a broken-down old bed, and a wobbly old table. At one end of his room there was a fireplace, and it had a fire burning—but the fire was just painted on the wall. Above the painted fire a painted kettle boiled merrily, sending forth a cloud of painted steam that looked quite real.

As soon as he reached the room, Geppetto got out his tools to start carving his puppet. But then he stopped to think.

"What name shall I give him?" he asked himself. "I know—I'll call him *Pinocchio*. It's a lucky name! I used to be friends with a whole family named Pinocchio: Papa Pinocchio, Mama Pinocchia, and all the little Pinocchi-kids. They made a wonderful living, that family. One of them became so rich he was a beggar!"

Now that he had found a name, Geppetto went right to

work on the puppet. Very quickly he carved the hair, then the forehead, and then the eyes.

Imagine how he felt when he saw the eyes move! And then they began staring at him.

Those two staring wooden eyes gave him a creepy feeling. He hated the feeling and asked, "Nasty eyes of wood, why do you stare at me so?"

But the eyes did not answer.

Next, he made the nose! And what a nose! It kept growing as soon as he carved it. It grew and grew and grew, and in just a few minutes he began to fear it would never stop.

Poor Geppetto tired himself out trying to shorten it. The more wood he cut away from it, the longer that bad-mannered nose grew.

After a while, he began carving a mouth.

Before he'd even finished it, though, the mouth began laughing and sneering.

"Stop being silly!" Geppetto shouted. He was furious by now, but he might as well have been shouting at the wall.

"I repeat! Stop being silly!" he roared in his most threatening voice.

The mouth stopped laughing and sneering. But now it stuck out its tongue as far as it could.

Geppetto was afraid he'd spoil his work if he paid any more attention to all this nonsense. So he pretended not to notice and went on with his carving.

He finished the mouth, and then made the puppet's chin, neck, shoulders, belly, arms, and hands.

As soon as the hands were done, he felt his wig being snatched off! He looked down, and what do you think he saw? It was his yellow wig in the puppet's brand-new hands.

"Pinocchio! Give that wig back to me!"

Instead of giving it back, Pinocchio stuck it on his own head. It almost smothered him, for it was so big it came down over his whole face.

The puppet's wildness made Geppetto terribly sad, sadder than he'd ever been before.

"You naughty little wretch!" he said. "I haven't even finished carving you and here you are, treating me, your own father, without any respect at all. Oh, that's bad, my boy, very bad!"

And he wiped away a tear from his eye.

He still hadn't made Pinocchio's legs and feet, and so he kept on carving.

No sooner had he finished the feet than one of them kicked him, right on the tip of his nose.

"It's my own fault," Geppetto said to himself. "I should have known what to expect. Well, well, it's too late now."

He picked the puppet up by the arms and set him down on the floor, to teach him to walk.

Pinocchio's legs were stiff and straight, and he didn't know how to use them. Geppetto held him by the hand and showed him how to move: first one foot, then the other.

Soon Pinocchio felt more comfortable walking. His legs relaxed, and he could take steps by himself. Then he began jumping all around the room. At last he shot out the door and sped down the street. He was running away from home!

Poor Geppetto chased after him, but couldn't catch him. Pinocchio was leaping and hopping like a wild hare. His little wooden feet clattered along the sidewalk, making as much noise as twenty men in heavy boots. He ran faster and faster.

"Grab him! Catch him!" shouted Geppetto. But the people on the street were terribly excited to see the wooden puppet tearing down the street like a racehorse. They

watched in delight and laughed and laughed, and kept laughing and laughing. I can't tell you how happy the sight made them.

At last, luckily, a policeman arrived. He had heard all the clatter and shouting, and at first he thought someone's pony must have broken away from its master. He planted

himself solidly in the middle of the street, with his legs wide apart, so that he could stop the runaway pony and quiet things down again.

Pinocchio saw the policeman blocking his way and decided to fool him by running right between his legs. That was a big mistake!

Deftly, without budging an inch, the policeman caught him by the nose. It was such a big, ridiculous nose that it seemed just made to be grabbed by policemen. He handed the puppet over to Geppetto, who had made up his mind to punish the little pest by boxing his ears. Imagine how embarrassed he was when he couldn't find Pinocchio's ears! Do you know why he couldn't? Because he'd been in such a hurry to finish making the puppet that he'd forgotten to carve them.

So now Geppetto took Pinocchio by the scruff of his neck and forced him to walk alongside him. Geppetto nodded fiercely and said, "At last we're going back home. When we get there, you can bet I'll make you pay for what you've done!"

At this Pinocchio flung himself to the ground and refused to go any further. All this time, of course, little groups of people with nothing better to do were gathering around and watching.

Some had one opinion. Some had another.

"Poor little puppet!" said some. "Who can blame him for not wanting to go home? Who knows what cruel things that awful Geppetto would do to him?"

Others had even worse things to say:

"Geppetto is supposed to be so nice. But he's very mean to children! If we let him keep that poor puppet, he'll probably chop him up into tiny pieces."

All in all, there was such a great fuss that the policeman set Pinocchio free and took poor old Geppetto off to jail. Geppetto couldn't think of the right words to defend himself. He could only moan like a calf. As he was led off to prison, he stammered and sobbed, "Wretched boy! And to think how hard I've tried to make him a nice young puppet! Well, it's all my fault. I should have known what to expect."

You wouldn't believe the things that happened afterwards. I'll tell you all about them soon.

CHAPTER

4

WELL, CHILDREN, I'M SORRY to tell you that when poor, innocent Geppetto was led off to jail our nasty little Pinocchio didn't care one bit. Once the policeman let him go he started running again. He dashed back home as fast as he could, cutting across people's fields and gardens. He bounded down steep, rocky hills, jumping over thorny hedges and wide ditches full of water, just like a young goat or like a young hare running away from hunters.

When he reached the house he found the door ajar. So he just pushed it open, went in, and then bolted it shut from the inside. Next, with a great sigh of relief, he went into Geppetto's room and sank down happily to rest on the floor.

But his contentment didn't last. Soon he heard someone, right there in the room with him, saying over and over:

"*Cri-cri-cri!*"

"Who's that?" cried Pinocchio, scared out of his wits.

"It's me."

Pinocchio turned around. A huge cricket was creeping up the wall.

"A *cricket*! Hey, who are you?"

"Just what you said—a cricket. I'm the Talking Cricket. I've lived in this very room for more than a hundred years."

"Oh, yeah?" said the puppet. "Well, now, this happens to be my room, and I don't want *you* hanging around all the time. Get out of here quick—and never come back!"

"Not so fast," said the Talking Cricket. "I'm not leaving—not until I tell you something you need to know."

"Okay, tell me. But hurry up about it!"

"It's this. Don't be one of those kids who fight with their parents and run away from home, and all for no good reason. Everything turns out wrong for them. Sooner or later they ruin their lives, and when it's too late they're sorry."

"Sing on, dumb old cricket, as long as you like. No matter what you say, I'm running away tomorrow morning, as soon as it's light. If I stayed here I'd have to do what all the other kids do—I'd have to go to school. They'd make me study and learn things. Not me! I'm not going to waste my time! What I want to do is chase butterflies and climb trees and steal baby birds out of nests!"

"You poor, silly little thing! Don't you know you'll grow up to be an absolutely perfect donkey if that's all you ever do? Everyone will pick on you and make fun of you and treat you like a fool."

"Shut up, you chirping old bad-luck cricket!" yelled Pinocchio.

But the Talking Cricket was patient and wise. He didn't lose his temper at these rude words. Instead, he went quietly on.

"You know, son, if you don't like the idea of school, why don't you at least learn some trade, like being a carpenter or maybe a plumber? That way you could always make an honest living."

"Want to hear my answer to *that*?" said Pinocchio, who was really growing very angry. "Of all the kinds of work in the world, there's just one kind I'd love to do."

"Good! A trade you'd like? Wonderful! What is it?"

"Eating and drinking and sleeping and having fun and living like a bum from morning to night."

"Uh-huh," said the Talking Cricket, as calm as ever. "For your information, my boy, just about everyone who follows that trade winds up in jail or a hospital."

"Hey! That's enough, old bad-luck croaker! If you make me any madder, too bad for you!"

"Poor little Pinocchio! I'm so sorry for you!"

"Sorry for *me*? Why?"

"Because you're only a foolish puppet, and—what's worse—you have a little wooden head."

At these words Pinocchio jumped up in a rage. He snatched a mallet from the workbench and hurled it at the Talking Cricket.

Probably he never really meant to hurt the Talking Cricket. But unfortunately the mallet hit him right on the head. He barely had the strength to chirp *"cri-cri-cri"* one last time. Then he was silent—all stiff, and squashed against the wall.

CHAPTER

MEANWHILE, IT WAS GETting dark. Pinocchio remembered that he hadn't eaten all day, and suddenly he felt a pang in his stomach that was very much like being hungry.

That feeling grows fast in children. A few minutes later he was *terribly* hungry. Then he became frantic, like a starving wolf.

Poor Pinocchio ran to the fireplace, where he saw a pot boiling. He reached out to lift the lid and see what was inside. But the pot, you remember, wasn't real but just painted on the wall. Oh, how lost Pinocchio felt standing there near that painted pot. And his nose, which was already too long, grew almost four inches longer.

He started rushing all around the room, poking in drawers and closets for a little bread—even if it was dry or stale—or a tiny crust, or a bone some dog hadn't wanted, or some moldy leftover pudding, or a fish bone, or a cherry pit, or anything at all he could just chew on. But he found nothing at all, a big nothing, just exactly nothing.

And meanwhile, he was growing hungrier and hungrier.

Poor Pinocchio could do nothing about it except yawn. His yawns were so huge that sometimes the corners of his mouth would touch his ears. And after yawning he had hiccups, and felt sick and weak.

He began to cry desperately, and he told himself, "Yes, the Talking Cricket was right. I was a bad boy to fight with my papa and run away from home. If my papa were only here now, I wouldn't be dying of yawns and hiccups. Oh, it's miserable to be hungry!"

Then, suddenly—a miracle! In a little pile of trash, he thought he saw something—something round and white, that looked very much like an egg! With one jump he had it in his hands. It was, really and truly, an egg!

I can't tell you how pleased that little puppet was. You'll have to imagine it for yourself. Still, he was a little afraid that he might only be dreaming. He shifted the egg from one hand to the other, and stroked it, and kissed it. And as he stroked and kissed it he muttered to himself:

"All right, now. How shall I cook it? Shall I make an omelet? . . . No, it would be better to poach it. . . . But wouldn't it taste better if I fried it? Or shouldn't I just boil it? No! The fastest way is best! I'll poach it in a little pan. I can't wait, I'm so hungry!"

Quickly he got hold of a brazier—a bowl that was full of red-hot coals—and put a pan on top of it to cook the egg in. He had no butter or oil, so he put some water in the pan instead. When the water began to steam, *crack!*—he broke the shell in two against the edge so that the egg could drop into the water.

But instead of the white and yolk of an egg, out hopped a tiny little chicken. It was extremely polite and cheerful and made an elegant bow as it said, "A thousand thanks, Mr.

Pinocchio, for saving me the work of breaking my shell my-self! So long! Stay healthy. Give my very best wishes to all my friends back home!"

With these words it spread its wings, flew out the open window, and was soon out of sight.

The poor puppet was stunned. He stood there as if under a spell, his eyes staring, his mouth open all the way, and the eggshell still in his hand. Then, after the first shock, he began to weep and scream and stamp his feet desperately.

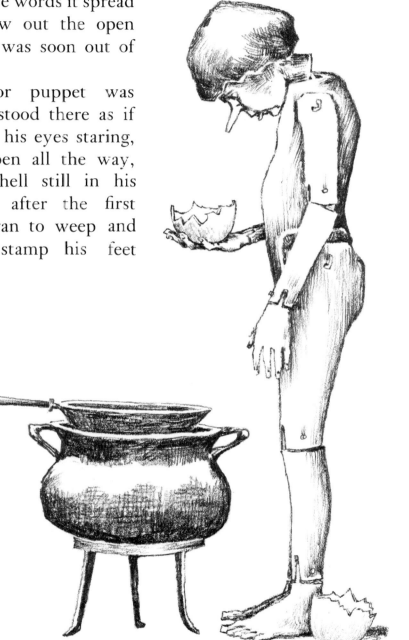

"Oh, how right the Talking Cricket was!" he wailed. "If only I hadn't run away from home, and if only my papa were here right now, I wouldn't be dying of hunger. Oh, how miserable it is to be hungry!"

His stomach was growling more and more painfully, and he didn't know how to make it stop. Finally he decided to leave the house and go out into the village. There, he hoped, he'd find some kind person who would give him a little bit of bread to eat.

CHAPTER

IT WAS A DREADFUL, STORMY, hellish night when Pinocchio rushed out looking for something to eat. Thunder rolled through the sky, louder and louder every minute. Lightning flashed as though the air were on fire. A cold, rough wind whistled savagely. It stirred up huge clouds of dust and shook the trees so hard they creaked.

Pinocchio was terribly afraid of thunder and lightning, but his hunger was stronger than his fear. So he dashed out into the storm, running faster and faster. He reached the village in a hundred jumps, panting like a hunting dog, with his tongue hanging out.

But he found the whole place dark and deserted. The shops were closed and so were the doors and windows of all the houses. You couldn't even see a dog anywhere. It seemed a village for dead persons, not living ones.

Pinocchio became wild with hunger and despair. He banged on someone's doorbell and then rang it without stopping.

"*This* will make somebody come to the door or window," he said to himself.

And an old man with a white nightcap on his head did come to the window, very grumpy.

"What do you want? It's late at night!" he shouted.

"Please, please. Would you give me just a tiny bit of bread?"

"Oh! Aha! Wait a moment! I'll be right back!" yelled the old man. He thought Pinocchio was part of a gang of troublesome boys who were always ringing doorbells and bothering nice, quiet people as they slept peacefully.

A moment later the window flew open and the old man's voice called out:

"Stand right underneath me and hold out your cap!"

Of course Pinocchio had no cap—not yet. But he stepped closer anyway, and stood under the window. *Splash!* A whole bucketful of water suddenly came down and soaked him from head to foot. You'd have thought he wasn't a puppet but a flowerpot full of thirsty geraniums.

So off ran poor Pinocchio again, dripping like a wet chick and all worn out with weariness and hunger. When he got home again he was too weak to remain standing even a moment longer. He sat down on a high stool in front of the warm brazier, which was still full of hot coals, and put his cold, wet, muddy feet up on top of it.

Ah, that was comfortable! He fell asleep at once. But while he slept, his little wooden feet caught fire. Very slowly, very quietly, they burned away and turned to ashes.

Pinocchio slept on, snoring loudly, as if his burning feet were somebody else's. Finally, just as the sun was rising, he woke up because someone was hammering at the door.

"Who's there?" he called out, rubbing his eyes and yawning.

"It's me!" said a voice.

The voice was Geppetto's.

CHAPTER

7

POOR LITTLE PINOCCHIO WAS still half asleep. His eyes hadn't yet opened wide enough to see that his feet had burned away. When he heard his papa's voice, he jumped from the stool to run and unlock the door. But, instead, he staggered this way and that three or four times, and then tripped and sprawled flat on the floor.

The clatter he made when he tripped and fell sounded the way a sack full of wooden spoons would sound if you dropped it to the sidewalk from the top of a very high building.

Out on the street, meanwhile, Geppetto was roaring, "Open up! Open up!"

"Dear Papa! I can't!" sobbed the puppet, weeping and bumping around on the floor.

"You can't? Why not?"

"Somebody ate up my feet!"

"Ate up your feet? Come on, who would do that?"

"The cat," said Pinocchio, who had just noticed Geppetto's pet cat amusing itself by making some wood chips dance between its forepaws.

"You open the door, I tell you!" Geppetto roared again. "If you don't, I'll teach you about cats once I do get in!"

"Papa, believe me! I can't get up! Oh, poor me! Poor me! I'll have to drag along on my knees all the rest of my life!"

Geppetto thought all these complaints were just one more silly trick of the puppet's. He decided to put an end to the nonsense, and clambered up the wall to the window.

He certainly was very angry. But then he saw his little puppet lying there helpless, really and truly with no feet, and his kind heart softened. He jumped down from the window into the room and caught Pinocchio up in his arms. He kissed him, gave him a thousand hugs, said all sorts of loving things to him, and, with big tears rolling down his cheeks, exclaimed, "My dear little Pinocchio, how in the world did you burn your feet off?"

"I don't know, Papa. But believe me, I've had such a long night of hell that I'll remember it for the rest of my life. There was thunder and lightning, and I was dying of hunger, and the Talking Cricket said, 'That's good—you've been bad and you deserve it.' So I said, 'You watch yourself, Cricket!' And he said, 'You're only a foolish little puppet, with a little wooden head.' And so I threw the mallet at him and he died. It was his own fault, because I didn't mean to kill him. I can prove it, because I put the pan on the brazier full of burning coals, but the little chicken flew out the window and said, 'So long, and best wishes to all my friends back home.' And I kept getting hungrier—and that's why the little old man in the nightcap said, 'Stand under the window and hold out your cap.' And there I was with that bucketful of water on my head because to beg for a crumb of bread isn't a disgrace, is it? And I ran right back here, and because I was so very hungry I put my feet on the brazier to dry them, and you came back, and I saw that my feet were burnt off, and all the time I kept getting hungrier and now I don't have feet any more! *Boo-hoo-hoo-hoo!*"

And poor Pinocchio cried and bellowed so loud that people could hear him three miles away.

Geppetto understood just one thing in this long, mixed-up speech: Pinocchio was dying of hunger. He pulled three pears out of his pocket and said, "I bought these three pears for my breakfast, but I want you to have them. Eat them. They'll make you feel a lot better."

"If you want me to eat them, please peel them first."

Geppetto was amazed. "Peel them?" he said. "I'd never have believed, my boy, that you were so picky about food. That's awful! In this world, from the time we're babies we have to get used to eating what we can get, and liking it, because we never know what might happen. Life is too full of surprises."

"You're right," said Pinocchio, "but I never eat fruit unless it's peeled. I hate biting the skin."

So that goodhearted Geppetto, with the patience of a saint, peeled the three pears with a paring knife and laid the peelings on a corner of the table.

Pinocchio swallowed the first pear in two mouthfuls. He was just going to throw away the core when Geppetto grabbed his arm and said, "No, don't throw it away! Everything in this world can be useful."

"Ugh—I'll never eat the core—never!" said the puppet in disgust. He looked and sounded as nasty as a viper.

"Who can tell?" said Geppetto, without letting himself get upset. "This world is full of surprises."

After a while the three cores, instead of being thrown

out the window, lay on the corner of the table alongside the peelings.

Having eaten—or rather, gulped down—the three pears, Pinocchio gave a great yawn and then complained, "I'm still hungry."

"Oh, my dear boy—but there's nothing left to give you."

"What? Nothing?"

"Only what's here on the table—these peelings and cores of the pears."

"Never mind!" said Pinocchio. "If there's nothing else, I'll have to take one of the skins."

So he took one and began chewing. At first he made a face, but then he finished off all the peelings, one after the other, in a flash. And then he did the same with the cores. He ate up every bit, patted his stomach contentedly, and said, in a gloating voice, "Mmm, now I feel fine."

"So then," observed Geppetto, "you see I was right when I told you not to be too picky and clever about what you eat. My dear boy, we never know what might happen in this world. Life has so many surprises!"

CHAPTER

Now pinocchio was no longer hungry, and so he began grumbling and crying about something else. He needed a new pair of feet!

But Geppetto still wanted to punish him for all his silly tricks. He let the puppet mope and fret for half a day and then said to him, "Why should I make new feet for you? Do you think I want to see you run away again?"

"I promise I'll be a good boy from now on," said the puppet, sobbing miserably.

"That's what all little boys say when they want something."

"And I promise I'll go to school, and I'll study, and I'll make you proud of me."

"That's what all little boys say when they want something."

"But I'm different from the other boys! I'm the best boy in the world, and I always tell the truth. I promise you, Papa. I'll learn a trade, and when you're old I'll be very nice to you and I'll take good care of you."

Geppetto had been acting very stern and strict. But his eyes filled with tears and his heart ached when he saw how pitiful Pinocchio looked. Without another word he gathered his tools together, picked out two especially good pieces of seasoned wood to carve, and set to work as hard as he could.

In less than an hour he had made a beautiful pair of little feet—tough, nimble, and restless. Believe me, only a great artist could have made a pair of feet like that!

Then Geppetto said, "Close your eyes and get some more sleep while I finish this job."

Pinocchio closed his eyes, but he was only pretending to go to sleep.

Geppetto mixed a tiny bit of glue in an eggshell, and with it he fastened the little wooden feet to Pinocchio's legs. He fastened them so neatly and perfectly that no one could ever tell they were only glued on.

As soon as the puppet realized he had brand-new feet, he sprang down from the table he'd been resting on and took a thousand wild jumps in the air and did a thousand somersaults. He felt crazy with happiness.

"I want to make up to you for everything you've done for me, Papa," he said. "I want to go to school right away!"

"That's my good little boy."

"But, if I do go, I'll need some clothes to wear."

Now Geppetto was so very poor that he didn't have even one penny in his pocket. But he made Pinocchio a little suit out of some paper that had pictures of flowers on it, and he made a pair of shoes out of the bark of a tree, and then he made a little white cap out of the soft inside part of a loaf of bread.

As soon as he put his new clothes on, Pinocchio ran to look at himself in the only mirror in the house—a basin full

of water. He was pleased with how he looked in the new clothes and strutted about like a contented peacock, shouting, "What a fine gentleman I am!"

"Of course you are," said Geppetto. "But remember—it's not fine clothes that make you a real gentleman, but being clean and neat."

"Oh," said the puppet, "by the way, there's one more thing I'll need for school, something I'll need more than anything else."

"Yes? And what's that?"

"I'll need a book, a primer, so I can learn my ABC's and how to spell."

"Yes, yes, you certainly do need an ABC book. But how will you get one?"

"Oh, that's easy! All you do is go to a bookshop and buy one."

"And the money? Where will I find that?"

"Don't ask me! I don't have any!"

"Neither do I," said the good old man, sitting down and looking very gloomy.

And Pinocchio, who was usually so lively and merry, became gloomy himself. Everyone, even a little boy, can understand how hard it is to be poor and needy.

"Hold on—just a minute!" cried Geppetto suddenly, leaping up in a great hurry. He threw on his old, worn-out jacket, full of patches and sewn-up holes, and shot out of the house.

Almost at once he was back again, with an ABC book in his hand for his little wooden son. But the jacket was gone. The poor man was wearing only a shirt and trousers, although it was cold outside and snowing.

"Papa! What have you done with your jacket?"

"I've sold it."

"Why did you sell it?"

"Because—because it made me too hot."

But Pinocchio understood the reason well enough. He couldn't help feeling a great flood of love in his heart. He jumped up, threw his arms around Geppetto's neck, and began kissing him all over his face.

CHAPTER

As soon as it stopped snowing, Pinocchio tucked his fine new ABC book under his arm and started out for school. While he walked he had a thousand different daydreams, each of them more wonderful than the last.

He repeated them to himself:

"Today at school I'll learn to read. Tomorrow I'll learn to write. The day after tomorrow I'll learn arithmetic. Then I'll know so much I can make all the money I want, and the first thing I'll do is buy my papa a fine new woolen jacket. Did I say a woolen jacket? No—I want it to be made of gold and silver, with diamond buttons! My poor papa certainly deserves it! To think he sold his old jacket to pay for my book and get me an education and is walking around shivering in his shirtsleeves, in this cold weather! Nobody but a papa would make a sacrifice like that."

While Pinocchio talked to himself in this excited way, he began to hear music being played far off—drumbeats and the sound of fifes: *tweedle-dee-dee, boom-boom-boom.*

He stopped and listened. The sounds were coming from

the end of a very long road that led away from the street he was on, where the school was, to a little village near the sea.

"What kind of music is that, I wonder. Too bad I have to go to school just now! If not . . ."

And he stood there, thinking. He was trying to make up his mind. Go to school? Or go hear the music?

At last the little wretch shrugged his shoulders. "Oh, well, I can go to school tomorrow. Today I'm going to listen to that music."

No sooner said than done. He turned the corner and began running very hard along that long road toward the sounds. The further he ran, the louder became the tune of the fifes and the beat of the drums: *tweedle-dee-dee, tweedle-dee-dee, boom-boom-boom.*

Suddenly he reached the middle of a great square full of people, all crowding around a big wooden pavilion covered with canvas and painted in bright colors.

"What's that building?" Pinocchio asked one of the little boys he saw in the crowd.

"See that poster up there? Just read it and you'll find out."

"I'd be glad to read it, but today I just don't happen to know how."

"Oh, boy, you must be stupid! All right, then, I'll read it for you. See those red letters that look like fire? They say: THE GREAT PUPPET THEATER!"

"Puppet theater! Is the show going on right now?"

"It's just starting."

"How much does it cost to go in?"

"Four pennies."

Pinocchio was in such a high fever of curiosity that he couldn't control himself. Without feeling shy at all, he asked, "Would you please lend me four pennies until tomorrow?"

"I'd be glad to lend you four pennies," said the boy, making fun of the way Pinocchio had talked to him, "but today I just don't happen to be able to."

"I'll give you my jacket for four pennies."

"Huh! What could I do with a jacket made of paper and covered with pictures of flowers? If I got caught in the rain and the jacket got wet, it would stick to me. I wouldn't even be able to take it off."

"Well, will you buy my shoes?"

"What? To start a fire with?"

"How much would you pay for my cap?"

"That would be something! A cap made of bread! Maybe the mice would come and nibble on it right on top of my head!"

Pinocchio was on pins and needles. He wanted to make one last offer, but didn't quite dare. He began to say something, then hesitated. He wasn't sure what to do, and felt guilty about even having such a thought. But finally he asked, "Will you pay me four pennies for this ABC book?"

"I'm just a little kid. I don't buy things from other kids," said the boy, who had more good sense than Pinocchio.

"I'll take your book for four pennies," said a man nearby who was selling old clothes. He had overheard the conversation.

And Pinocchio sold it to him right then and there. To think that poor old Geppetto had to stay home in his shirt-sleeves shivering from the cold, because he had bought that ABC book for his little son!

CHAPTER

10

WHEN PINOCCHIO FINALLY got into the puppet theater, something happened. He stirred up a small revolution!

You see, the curtain had already gone up on stage. The play had begun.

Punch and Judy had rushed in at the same time and bumped into each other. As usual, they were shouting angrily, "I'll box your ears!" "I'll slap you over the head with my big stick!" Then other puppets joined in, screaming and fighting.

The audience loved it all. They laughed so hard their stomachs hurt when they saw those puppets quarreling and waving their arms about and insulting each other, just as though they were real people and about as reasonable as human beings usually are!

Then, suddenly, one of the puppets—Harlequin—stopped his screaming and leaping about. He turned and looked out over the audience, pointed his finger at someone, and cried out with enormous excitement:

"Ye gods in heaven above! Am I dreaming? Am I

awake? Surely . . . surely . . . that . . . must be . . . yes, must be . . . Pinocchio down there!"

"Yes! Yes!" shouted Punch. "Yes! It's he! It's him! It's Pinocchio!"

"It is! It is!" shrieked Madam Rose, poking her head out from behind the scenery. "It's Pinocchio!"

"It's Pinocchio! It's Pinocchio!" howled all the puppets together, jumping to the front of the stage from everywhere. "It's Pinocchio! Our brother Pinocchio! Hurrah for Pinocchio!"

"Pinocchio!" called Harlequin. "Jump up here with us! Come up and throw yourself into the arms of your wooden brothers and sisters!"

At this loving call, Pinocchio made three great leaps. The first one took him from the back of the theater to the front row. The second took him from the front row to the top of the orchestra conductor's head. The third took him right up to the stage.

I can't describe all the hugs and kisses, the squeezing, the love pinches and friendly punches all those good, true brother and sister puppets gave Pinocchio, and all the happy confusion and wild enthusiasm of those tree-people, the wooden actors and actresses in their theater.

It was all very heartwarming, of course. And yet the audience in the seats, who had come to see a play, grew impatient and began to shout, "We want the show! We want the show!"

They were wasting their breath. No one listened. The puppets, instead of going on with the show, made twice as much noise and went twice as wild. They hoisted Pinocchio on their shoulders and bore him in triumph down to the footlights.

Just then the puppet master turned up on the stage. He was an ogre, so big and ugly it would scare you just to look at him. His ink-black beard was so long it dragged along the ground. Whenever he walked, he stepped on it and tripped over it. His mouth was as huge as an open furnace. His eyes were like two great red lanterns, with a flame burning in each of them. He carried an enormous, frightful whip that he cracked again and again; it was made of live snakes and foxes' tails, all twisted together.

What a shock! Quickly everybody grew so still you

could have heard a fly's wings moving in the air. The poor terrified little puppets—all those wooden actors and actresses—were shaking like leaves in the wind.

"What's all this excitement in my theater?" thundered the puppet master, looking at Pinocchio. "Why are you making all this trouble?" He sounded like the Devil, if the Devil ever had a bad cold in his head.

"Please, your honor! It's not my fault!"

"Shut up! I'll take care of you tonight!"

And he lifted Pinocchio into the air and hung him from a nail in the kitchen, where a fine fat sheep was turning slowly on a spit for the ogre's supper. Later, when the play was over, the puppet master went back into the kitchen to see how well the sheep was being roasted. He found the fire very low, and saw that not enough wood remained in it to finish browning the roast properly. So the puppet master roared out a command to Punch and Harlequin:

"Bring me that puppet over there—the one hanging on the nail. He seems to be made of very good wood—very dry. When I throw him into the fire, I'm sure he'll blaze right up and finish roasting my sheep beautifully."

Harlequin and Punch didn't move. But Fire-eater gave them one terrible look which made them shake with fear. They rushed over to Pinocchio, pulled him down, and dragged him back with them. He wriggled and squirmed like an eel out of water, screaming all the while:

"Papa! Save me! I don't want to die! I don't want to die!"

CHAPTER

11

FIRE-EATER, THE PUPPET master, certainly was terrifying, especially with that beard of his that hung down like an enormous black apron over his chest and legs. I can't deny it. And yet he really wasn't so bad, as we can see by what happened when poor Pinocchio was dragged before him, struggling and kicking and screaming, "I don't want to die! I don't want to die!" Fire-eater was touched and began to feel sorry for him. For about a minute he was able to stay angry, but he couldn't continue it, no matter how hard he tried. Finally, he gave a mighty sneeze!

Until then Harlequin had been standing nearby, grieving and bent over like a weeping willow tree. But when he heard that sneeze, Harlequin suddenly grinned happily and, whispering softly, leaned toward Pinocchio.

"Good news, brother! Good news! When Fire-eater sneezes it's a sign he's taken pity on you! You're safe!"

You know that when ordinary people are sorry for somebody they usually cry. Or at least they pretend to cry, and act as though they're wiping tears from their eyes. Well,

Fire-eater was different. He had the habit of sneezing when he was moved to pity. That was his one way of showing how he felt deep in his heart.

Yet after he sneezed he still sounded rough and ugly and mean. In his horrible voice he roared at Pinocchio:

"Quit all that crying! All your complaining has given me a howling pain here in the pit of my stomach! I feel a spasm of pain that almost . . . almost . . . *Ah-choo! Ah-choo!*" And then he sneezed twice more.

"Bless you!" said Pinocchio.

"Thank you! Are your papa and mama still alive?"

"My papa—yes. I never knew my mama."

"How sad it would have been for your poor old papa if I'd thrown you among those burning coals! Poor old man! I'm so sorry for him! *Ah-choo! Ah-choo! Ah-choo!*" And he sneezed three times again.

"Bless you!" said Pinocchio.

"Thank you! At the same time, you should be sorry for me, too. Now I haven't any wood to finish roasting that sheep! Believe me, you'd have been pretty useful for that—but never mind. I've taken pity on you, and so I'll just have to be patient. Instead of burning you in the fire, I'll have to use one of my own puppets. Attention, police!"

At this strange command two wooden policemen appeared. They were extremely tall and extremely skinny.

They wore old-fashioned cocked hats and were waving gigantic swords.

The puppet master roared out more commands to them in his rumbling, wheezing voice.

"Grab hold of that Harlequin over there. Tie him up and throw him into the fire. I'm hungry and I want my sheep well roasted!"

Imagine how poor Harlequin felt! He was so frightened that his knees buckled under him, and he fell flat on his face.

Pinocchio's heart began to pound at this sight. He threw himself at the puppet master's feet and, shedding tears like rain, soaked his whole long beard from top to bottom. And as he wept he pleaded, "Have mercy, dear good Lord Fire-eater!"

"We don't have any lords around here!" said the puppet master angrily.

"Have pity, noble knight!"

"Don't have any knights here, either!"

"Have pity, mighty general!"

"No generals here, either!"

"Then have pity, Your Excellency!"

When he heard that word "Excellency," the puppet master suddenly broke into a happy smile. He became altogether more human and gentle and asked, "Well, my boy, what would you like me to do now?"

"All I want is one thing. Please set poor Harlequin free!"

"But that's impossible. Now that I've let *you* go, you see, I have to throw *him* in the fire. You know I want my sheep to be well roasted!"

"In that case," cried Pinocchio, rising to his full height and throwing his little cap made of bread to the floor, "in that case, I know what my duty is. Come on, you policemen! Tie me up and throw me into the fire. No—it would be all wrong if my true friend, poor Harlequin, had to die in my place."

These words, which Pinocchio spoke loudly and boldly, like a real hero, made all the puppets, who were standing around and listening, burst into tears. Even the wooden policemen cried like baby lambs.

At first Fire-eater remained as hard and cold as a block of ice. Then, little by little, he began melting and sneezing. After the fifth sneeze, he opened his arms to Pinocchio and rumbled, "You're a fine, brave lad. Come here and give me a kiss."

Pinocchio ran to him and clambered up his beard like a squirrel. Then he planted a noisy kiss on the tip of Fire-eater's nose.

"Then . . . my life . . . is it spared?" asked poor Harlequin in a voice so faint you could hardly hear it.

"Your life is spared!" answered Fire-eater. Sighing and shaking his head, he added, "Patience! Tonight I'll just have to have my roast sheep half raw. But next time—woe to whoever comes along!"

When they heard that Harlequin wasn't going to be burned, the puppets all ran up onto the stage to celebrate. They lighted the lamps and chandeliers and began leaping about and dancing. When dawn came, they were still leaping and dancing.

CHAPTER

12

THE NEXT DAY FIRE-EATER called Pinocchio to him and asked, "What's your papa's name?"

"Geppetto."

"And what kind of work does he do?"

"His work is being poor."

"Does he make much money?"

"He makes enough never to have a penny in his pocket. Just think! To buy me my ABC book for school he had to sell the only jacket he had—the one he was wearing. It was so full of holes and patches it hurt me to look at it."

"Poor devil! I almost feel sorry for him. Here, take these five gold coins. Give them to him right away, and also give him my best wishes."

As you can imagine, Pinocchio thanked the puppet master a thousand times. He hugged all the puppets of the company, one by one—even the wooden policemen. Then, dizzy with joy, he set off for home.

He'd gone only a few hundred yards when he met a Fox with a lame leg and a Cat that was blind in both eyes. They were walking along slowly, helping one another as they went, like friends sharing each other's misery. Since the Fox was lame, he leaned on the Cat. And since the Cat was blind, he let the Fox lead the way.

"Good morning, Pinocchio," said the Fox politely.

"How did you learn my name?" asked the puppet.

"I know your papa well."

"Where did you see him?"

"Standing at the door of his house, just yesterday."

"What was he doing?"

"He was shivering with cold, in his shirtsleeves."

"My poor papa! But from now on, with God's help, he'll never shiver again!"

"Really? Why is that?"

"Because I'm now a rich man!"

"You? A rich man?" said the Fox. He gave a nasty, sneering laugh. The Cat laughed too, but pretended to be combing his whiskers with his forepaws so Pinocchio wouldn't notice.

"What are you laughing at?" cried Pinocchio. "I'm sorry if this makes your mouth water, but I'll bet these five very beautiful gold coins will help you understand."

And he reached into his pocket, pulled out the coins Fire-eater had given him, and jingled them in his hand.

The sound of the money was so pleasing that the Fox couldn't help stretching out his paw—the one that was supposed to be lame—for a moment. And the Cat opened his eyes so wide they looked like green lights, but then he closed them again before Pinocchio could notice.

"Yes," said the Fox, "and now what do you plan to do with your golden coins?"

"That's easy! First of all, I'll buy my papa a fine new jacket, all gold and silver and with diamond buttons. And right after that I'll buy a brand-new book of ABC's."

"For yourself?"

"Right. I want to go to school and be a good student."

"But look at me," said the Fox. "Because I had such a stupid love of studying, I went lame in one leg."

"Yes, and look at me," said the Cat. "Because I had such a stupid love of studying, I went blind in both eyes."

At that moment a white blackbird that had been perched on a hedge near the roadside sang out sweetly and

said, "Pinocchio, don't listen to those liars! If you do you'll be sorry!"

The poor blackbird! If only he hadn't said anything! With a sudden jump, the Cat pounced on him and—without giving him time to say "Oh!"—swallowed him, feathers and all, at one gulp.

After this quick little meal he wiped his mouth, closed his eyes again, and once more pretended he was blind.

"Poor blackbird!" said Pinocchio. "Why were you so cruel to him, Mr. Cat?"

"I did it to teach him a lesson, once and for all. Next time he'll know better than to stick his beak into other people's conversations."

By now they were more than halfway to Geppetto's house. Suddenly the Fox stopped and said, "Would you like to have twice as many gold coins as you've got now?"

"What?"

"Would you like those five miserable old coins of yours to turn into a hundred, or a thousand, or two thousand coins?"

"Wouldn't I?" said Pinocchio. "But how?"

"It's simple. Don't go straight home now. Come along with us instead."

"But where are you going?"

"We're on our way to Foolville."

Pinocchio stood thinking for a while. But then he spoke up firmly.

"No, I can't do it. I'm too close to home right now, and that's where I want to go. My papa's waiting for me. Poor old man, who knows how miserable I made him by not coming right back home? I've been a bad boy for a long time—too long. The Talking Cricket was right when he warned me. He said, 'Disobedient boys never have any luck.' I've tested that, all right, and my luck has certainly been bad. Even last night, in Fire-eater's house, I was in great danger . . . *Br-r-r!* It makes my hair stand on end just to think about it!"

"So, then," said the Fox, "you've really decided to go home? All right, then, go ahead! So much the worse for you!"

"So much the worse for you!" echoed the Cat.

"Think it over, Pinocchio. You're just kicking away a fortune."

"A fortune!" echoed the Cat.

"Just think! By tomorrow morning your five gold pieces can grow into two thousand."

"Two thousand!" echoed the Cat.

"That much? But how can it be?" cried Pinocchio, whose mouth had fallen wide open in surprise.

"It's easy enough to explain," said the Fox. "I guess you know that in Foolville there's a magic meadow called the Field of Miracles. You dig a little hole in the ground there and—for example—put a gold piece into it. Then you fill up the hole again, pour two bucketfuls of water from the fountain over it, add a pinch of salt, and, in the evening, go quietly to bed. While you're asleep the coin sprouts and grows. The next morning you get up and run back to the magic meadow—and what do you find? I'll tell you what! A beautiful tree, loaded with as many bright new golden coins as there are kernels in an ear of corn!"

While the Fox talked Pinocchio's eyes grew bigger and bigger with wonder. He was so amazed that his head was swimming.

"So then," he shouted, "if I bury my five gold pieces in that field tonight, how many will I find growing tomorrow morning?"

"That's easy, too," said the Fox. "You can figure it out on the tips of your fingers. Now, suppose that each coin you plant grows into a bunch of five hundred coins overnight. All right. Just multiply that five hundred by five. That makes twenty-five hundred. So then, tomorrow morning you'll find yourself with twenty-five hundred gold coins weighing down your pockets."

"Whew!" cried Pinocchio, dancing about with excitement. "What a wonderful thing! After I gather my bunches of coins, I'll keep four of them for myself and give the fifth bunch of five hundred coins to you and Mr. Cat as a reward."

"A reward—for us?" growled the Fox angrily. "God forbid!"

"Forbid!" echoed the Cat.

"We never work for anything as disgusting as money," said the Fox. "We only work to bring happiness to others."

"Others!" echoed the Cat.

"What nice people!" thought Pinocchio. And now he forgot about his papa, and the new jacket, and the ABC book, and all the good things he had decided. He had just one thing to say to the Fox and the Cat:

"Come on! Let's go, right now!"

CHAPTER

AND OFF THEY WENT. THEY walked and walked and walked, on and on, until it was night. And then they still kept walking. At last, dead tired, they reached the Red Crab Inn.

"Let's stop and rest here for a while," said the Fox. "We can get something to eat and then sleep for a few hours. At midnight we can get up and start out again, and by dawn we'll be there—in the Field of Miracles."

They went inside and sat down at a table, although none of them felt really hungry. They were far too tired to eat much.

The poor Cat had a terrible stomachache. He couldn't eat a thing except thirty-five fish covered with tomato sauce and four helpings of tripe covered with melted butter and Parmesan cheese. (The tripe didn't taste just right to him, and so he ordered more butter and cheese three separate times!)

The poor Fox would have liked to nibble just a tiny bit, like the Cat. But he wasn't well and his doctor had put him

on a special diet—only the smallest amount of very plain food. And so he had to be content with a hare baked in sweet-and-sour sauce and surrounded by four fat, tender, young roasted chickens. Then, as a between-course appetizer, he ordered a fricassee made of partridges, rabbits, frogs, lizards, and sweet grapes flavored with egg sauce. But then he simply wasn't able to touch another thing. Even to look at food, he said, made him sick to his stomach; he couldn't dream of actually putting any in his mouth.

As for Pinocchio, he ate the least of all. He asked the waiter to bring him half a walnut and the little bit of crust at the end of a loaf of bread, but then he just left the food on his plate. The poor lad thought about only one thing: the Field of Miracles. He had indigestion of the brain, because his mind was crammed with all the gold coins he was imagining.

When dinner was over, the Fox went over to the innkeeper and said, "We'd like two nice rooms—one for Mr. Pinocchio and one for me and my partner, Mr. Cat. We'd like a few hours of sleep, but please remember to wake us up at midnight so we can go on with our journey."

"Yes, sir!" said the innkeeper, smiling. He winked at the Fox and the Cat as if to say, "I get it—I know what you're doing. Don't worry. I won't tell on you."

The moment Pinocchio was in bed he fell fast asleep and began dreaming. He dreamt he was in the middle of a meadow, and the meadow was full of little trees whose branches were heavy with bunches of gold coins swinging in the wind. They made such a friendly, jingling sound— *ching, ching, ching*—as if they were calling out: "Whoever wants us, *ching*, come and take us, *ching, ching, ching*!" In the dream everything was perfect, and Pinocchio was just reaching out to take a handful of those lovely coins and put them in his pocket. But all of a sudden he was awakened by three heavy knocks on his door.

It was the innkeeper, who had come to tell him it was now midnight.

"Are my friends ready?" asked the puppet.

"More than ready! They left two hours ago."

"Two hours ago! Why were they in such a hurry?"

"Because of Mr. Cat. He received a message that his oldest kitten's life is in danger because of sore feet."

"Oh! I'm sorry. I suppose they paid the bill for our dinner?"

"What do you mean, sir? They're far too polite to insult a fine gentleman like you by not letting you pay the bill!"

"Hmm! Too bad! That's the kind of insult I wouldn't mind getting!" said Pinocchio, scratching his puzzled head. "And by the way—where did these dear, polite friends of mine say they'd meet me?"

"In the Field of Miracles, tomorrow morning at dawn."

It cost Pinocchio one of his gold coins to pay for the dinner. He gave the innkeeper the money and started out.

Or rather, he groped his way. Outside the inn the night was so black he couldn't see at all. And it was so still he couldn't hear a leaf rustle. The only things that moved were certain night birds of prey flying across the road from one hedge to another. Sometimes their flapping wings brushed against Pinocchio's nose, and he would jump back and cry out with fright.

"Who's that?"

From far away he would hear an echo repeated again and again from the surrounding hills:

"Who's that? Who's that? Who's that?"

Pinocchio kept walking. Soon he saw a tiny creature on a tree trunk. It shone with a faint glow, like the flame inside a porcelain lamp.

"Who are you, little creature?" asked Pinocchio.

"I'm the ghost of the Talking Cricket," said a weak, weak voice that seemed to come from another world.

"Why are you here?" said the puppet.

"I've come to give you some advice you need. Turn around and go home now. Give the four gold coins you have left to your poor papa. He's all alone there, weeping in despair because he hasn't seen you since the morning you started off for school."

"But tomorrow my papa will be rich! My four gold coins are going to grow into two thousand coins!"

"No, my poor boy! Don't ever trust somebody who promises to make you rich in a hurry, between sunrise and sunset. People like that are either crazy or crooks. Listen to me—do you hear? Turn around right now and march straight home."

"Not me! I'm going straight ahead."

"Don't you realize what time it is? The night is fearful and dark and long."

"I'm going straight ahead."

"The road is dangerous."

"I'm going straight ahead."

"Remember: boys who don't listen to others and always

want their own way get into terrible trouble. Sooner or later, they always do!"

"The same old story. Good night, old Cricket."

"Good night, Pinocchio—and may heaven save you from the dampness of night and the murderers somewhere out there."

With these words the Talking Cricket disappeared, like a candle flame suddenly blown out by the wind, and the road became even darker than before.

CHAPTER

14

"HUH! PEOPLE ARE ALWAYS making all kinds of trouble for us kids!" grumbled Pinocchio as he started groping his way down the dark road again. "Everybody scolds us. Everybody warns us. Everybody keeps telling us what to do. Why, to hear them talk you'd think they all—even the Talking Cricket—were either my papa or my teacher! Just because I didn't want to listen to that dumb old Cricket, look at what he said to me! Who knows how much bad luck, according to him, I'm going to have? He even said I'd meet murderers on this road. It's a good thing I don't happen to believe in murderers! They're just make-believe people that our papas invent so we'll be too scared to go out walking at night. But anyway, suppose I do happen to meet some murderers tonight—think I'd be scared? Not me! Not even in a dream! I'll just look them in the eye and shout, 'Hey, murderers, what do *you* want? Just remember: nobody fools around with *me*! Mind your own business and get away from me! You heard me—shut up and go away!' Once they see how tough I am, those silly murderers will blow away faster than the wind. I can see them running now! And if they're too stupid to run away themselves, then I'll run instead and get rid of them that way."

But Pinocchio's brave thoughts stopped suddenly, for he thought he heard a faint rustling of leaves behind him.

He turned to have a look. There, through the blackness, he could see two ugly dark figures. They had sacks over their heads. Hopping swiftly on tiptoe behind him, they looked like strange shadows or ghosts. One was tall; the other was short.

"It's the murderers!" Pinocchio said to himself. Quickly he stuck his four gold coins into his mouth and pressed them firmly under his tongue. Then he made a great leap and started running as fast as he could. But before he could even touch ground again after that leap, he was grabbed from behind and heard two gruff, deep voices threatening, "Your money or your life!"

Pinocchio couldn't speak, because he was holding the gold coins under his tongue. Instead, he bowed and made all sorts of faces and waved his arms about. He was trying to show the two disguised robbers, whose eyes he could see through the holes in the sacks they were wearing, that he was only a poor puppet and didn't have even a false penny in his pockets.

"Quit your clowning and hand over the money!" shouted the murderers savagely.

The puppet shook his head and opened out the palms of his hands as if to say, "Sorry, I don't have any money."

"Hand it over, or we'll kill you!" growled the tall murderer.

"We'll kill you!" echoed the short murderer.

"And after we kill you, we'll kill your papa!"

"No! No! No! Not my poor father!" cried Pinocchio unhappily. And as soon as he spoke the gold coins went *clank!* in his mouth.

"Oho, you little wretch! So you had the money tucked under your tongue all the time! All right now, spit it out!"

But as we know, Pinocchio was stubborn!

"So—pretending to be deaf, are you? Hold on a moment, then. We'll find the way to make you spit out your gold!"

And indeed they tried. One of them grabbed the end of the puppet's nose and yanked it upward cruelly. The other got hold of his chin, pulling it downward with all his force.

But it didn't work. Pinocchio's mouth seemed to be nailed shut, and his lips seemed clamped together.

The short murderer pulled out a huge, vicious-looking knife. He tried to force it between Pinocchio's lips and pry them open. Quick as a flash, Pinocchio seized the murderer's hand between his teeth, bit it clean off, and spat it out. Imagine his surprise when, instead of a hand, he saw that he had spat a cat's paw to the ground!

Now Pinocchio grew full of courage. He tore at the murderers with his sharp little wooden nails and broke loose from them, jumping over some bushes beside the road and dashing over the fields. The murderers chased after him like two dogs after a hare. The one that had lost a paw ran on only one leg, though I can't tell you how in the world he did it.

After running madly for about nine miles, Pinocchio couldn't run another step. He was sure they'd catch him now. He climbed to the top of a very tall pine tree and sat on the highest branch. The murderers tried to climb up after him, but halfway up the trunk they slipped and fell back to the ground, skinning their hands and feet painfully.

But they wouldn't give up. Now they piled some dry wood at the foot of the tree and set fire to it. In a second, the tree started burning and then blazed up like a candle in the wind. Pinocchio watched the flames rising higher and higher toward him and decided he didn't want to end up like a roasted pigeon. So he let himself drop from the treetop and again began running through fields and vineyards. The murderers stayed right behind him, very close, without ever getting tired.

By now it was almost morning. All three of them were still running, but suddenly Pinocchio was blocked by a very wide and deep ditch. It was full of filthy, brown water that looked exactly like coffee with milk in it. What could Pinocchio do now? He gave a great shout—"One! Two! Three!"—and, with one mighty effort, sprang over the ditch. The murderers tried the same thing but didn't judge the distance properly and—*bang! thud! splash!*—they came down right in the middle of the ditch. Pinocchio heard them splashing and thrashing about in the water, and as he kept running he laughed and shouted, "Have a nice bath, my noble murderers!"

In fact, he was sure they were drowning. But when he looked behind him a little later, he saw them still chasing after him. Their faces were still masked by their ghostly looking sacks, and they were both dripping water like two cracked buckets.

CHAPTER

15

THE PUPPET STOPPED AND looked around hopelessly. He felt like dropping to the ground and giving up. But then, suddenly, he saw something—a snow-white cottage—gleaming far away in the dark green woods.

"Do I have enough strength left to get to that house before I collapse?" he wondered to himself. "Maybe I do! Maybe I'll be all right!"

Without a second's hesitation he shot off again, at full speed, toward the woods. And the murderers were right at his heels.

After running desperately for almost two hours, he finally reached the cottage. He was almost too weak to knock, but he managed to tap at the door.

Nobody answered.

He took a deep breath and knocked again, very hard. He could hear his enemies' pounding feet and their heavy gasps of breath.

Still no answer.

It was no use knocking. In his panic, Pinocchio started

kicking the door and butting it with his head. Soon a beautiful little girl appeared at the window. Her hair was blue and her face was as white as a statue's. Her eyes were shut and her hands were crossed over her heart. Then she spoke, without moving her lips, in a voice that seemed to come from another world.

"There's nobody in this house. They've all died."

"But what about you? Can't you, at least, let me in quickly?" cried Pinocchio, weeping miserably.

"I have died too."

"You? Then why is it you're standing at the window?"

"I'm waiting for my coffin. They're bringing it to take me away in it."

As soon as she said these words, the little girl disappeared. The window closed itself without a sound.

"Oh, beautiful little girl with your blue hair," cried Pinocchio, "please have pity on me and open the door! Have pity on a poor boy who's being chased by mur—"

Before he could finish saying "murderers" he was grabbed by the neck. Once again he heard those same two savage voices growling.

"This time you won't get away!"

The puppet saw death flash before his eyes. He trembled so violently that his wooden knees rattled together. So did the four golden coins he still held under his tongue.

"All right," shouted the murderers together, "will you open up your mouth now—yes or no? Oho, so you won't answer! Fine! Then it's up to us. Don't worry, we'll open it for you!"

They drew out two long, terrifying knives, sharp as razors, and—*oof!*—they both stabbed him in the stomach at the same time.

Luckily, our puppet was made of very hard wood. The knives shattered into a thousand tiny bits. The murderers stood there amazed, staring at each other, with nothing in their hands but their knife handles.

"I get it!" said one of them. "Since our knives are no use, we'll have to hang him. Yes, let's hang him at once."

No sooner said than done. They tied his hands behind his back, tied a rope around his neck, and hanged him from the highest branch of an enormous tree called the Big Oak.

After that they rested. They sat down on the grass and watched Pinocchio thrashing about in the air. They were waiting for him to stop his kicking and jerking and die. But after three hours his eyes remained wide open, his mouth remained clamped shut, and he was kicking and thrashing about more than ever.

At last they grew tired of all this waiting. They looked up at Pinocchio and sneered, "So long until tomorrow! When

we get back, let's hope you'll have the good manners to be dead by then—with your mouth finally open!"

And off they went.

Meanwhile, a stormy north wind had sprung up, roaring and whistling in a great fury. It battered the poor puppet about, making him swing violently, like a church bell ringing on a holiday. This hurt his whole body dreadfully, and the noose around his neck grew tighter and tighter so that he couldn't breathe.

Little by little, his eyes grew dull and he felt death coming nearer and nearer. But he still kept hoping some kind soul would come and save him. Then, after waiting and waiting, he saw that nobody would appear—nobody at all. His poor papa came into his mind and, nearly dead now, Pinocchio stammered out:

"Oh, my dear Papa! If only you were here!"

His breath was all gone. He could speak no more. His eyes closed, his mouth fell open, his legs grew straighter and straighter. Then, after a great shudder, he hung there, stiff and still.

CHAPTER

16

So THERE WAS POOR PINOC-chio, hanged by those mur-derers from the highest branch of the Big Oak. He dangled there, bouncing about in the blasts of the cold north wind as though he were dancing. Yet even so he looked more dead than alive. The beautiful little blue-haired girl came to her window again and saw him dangling and bouncing in the air. Her heart was filled with pity. Gently, she clapped her hands together three times.

At once there was a noisy whirr of wings. A huge falcon came whizzing through the air and perched on the window-sill.

"What is your wish, gracious Blue Fairy?" he asked, dipping his beak in deep respect. (For I must tell you: that beautiful little blue-haired girl was really a very kind fairy, who had lived there in the woods for more than a thousand years.)

"Do you see that puppet dangling from the highest branch of the Big Oak?"

"Yes, I see him."

"Very good. Please fly over to him and untie the rope around his neck with that powerful beak of yours. Then lay him down, ever so carefully, on the grass at the foot of the tree."

The falcon flew off. In two minutes he was back, saying, "I've done it!"

"And how did he look to you? Is he alive or is he dead?"

"He *looked* quite dead. But he can't really be! When I untied the rope around his neck he let out a sigh and, in a weak little voice, he croaked: 'I . . . feel . . . a . . . little . . . better . . . now.'"

The Blue Fairy clapped her hands together twice. In came a magnificent poodle, walking on his hind legs like a human being. His name was Medoro.

The poodle was all dressed up in a splendid uniform, like a coachman for a king or queen. On his head he wore a beautiful old-fashioned three-cornered hat with gold braid around it. Under the hat he wore a big curly white wig that flopped down to his shoulders. And he was also wearing a chocolate-colored jacket with diamond buttons and two enormous pockets to hold the bones his mistress gave him during dinner, and a pair of short red velvet breeches, and silk stockings, and little shoes that just fit his paws. Behind him hung a kind of small umbrella case made of blue satin. Whenever it rained he would tuck his tail into it.

"Hurry, my brave Medoro!" said the Blue Fairy to the poodle. "Go at once and harness up the finest carriage in my coach house and drive it straight to the woods. When you reach the Big Oak, you'll see a poor little puppet stretched out half dead on the grass. Lift him up gently, lay him tenderly on the seat cushions of the carriage, and bring him to me immediately. Do you understand?"

To show he did understand, the poodle tucked his tail into his blue satin tail case and wagged it three or four times. Then he sped off like a racehorse.

A second later the most beautiful little carriage you ever saw shot out of the coach house. It was the color of misty air. Its cushions were stuffed with canary feathers. Its inside was lined with whipped cream and decorated with custard and cookies. The little carriage was drawn by a hundred pairs of white mice, and the poodle sat high on the driver's seat urging them forward. He cracked his whip impatiently, first left and then right, for fear he would arrive too late.

In less than fifteen minutes the little carriage was back. The Blue Fairy, who stood waiting at the door, lifted the poor puppet in her arms and carried him into a little room whose walls were made of mother-of-pearl. She laid Pinocchio carefully down on the bed there. And then she sent for the most famous doctors that could be found nearby.

The doctors arrived quickly, one right after the other—first a crow, then a screech owl, and then the Talking Cricket.

"I want your opinion, gentlemen," said the Blue Fairy to these three doctors gathered around Pinocchio's bed. "Please tell me: Is this poor little puppet alive or is he dead?"

The crow stepped forward. He felt Pinocchio's pulse, then his nose, and then the little toe of each foot. When he had felt them completely, he solemnly pronounced these words:

"In my opinion, this puppet is certainly dead. But if, after all, he has the bad luck not to be dead, then that's a sure sign he must still be alive!"

"I'm sorry, indeed," said the screech owl, "to have to disagree with my famous friend and colleague, Dr. Crow. In my opinion, however, this puppet is still alive. But if, after all, he has the bad luck not to be alive, then that's a sure sign he must be dead!"

"And what's your opinion?" said the Blue Fairy to the Talking Cricket. "Don't you have anything to say?"

"In my opinion, a doctor who doesn't know what to say ought to keep quiet. But there's something I *can* tell you. I happen to recognize this puppet. I've known him quite a while!"

Pinocchio, who until now had been lying as still as some ordinary piece of wood, suddenly began to shiver and shudder so hard that he made the whole bed shake.

"That puppet lying there," continued the Talking Cricket, "has been a pretty naughty little rascal for quite a long time!"

Pinocchio opened his eyes and then quickly closed them again.

"He's a lazy, good-for-nothing little monster."

Pinocchio buried his face under the sheets.

"That puppet is a wicked, disobedient child who will make his poor papa die of a broken heart."

A muffled outburst of crying and sobbing exploded in the room. Imagine everyone's surprise when they lifted the sheet and saw that the crying and sobbing came from Pinocchio!

"When a dead person cries and sobs, it must be a sure sign he's getting better," pronounced the crow solemnly.

"I'm sorry to contradict my illustrious friend and colleague," replied the screech owl. "In my opinion, however, when a dead person cries and sobs it must be a sure sign he doesn't like being dead."

CHAPTER

17

As soon as the doctors left the room, the Blue Fairy went over to Pinocchio's bed and felt his forehead. It was hot. He was running a terribly high fever.

She mixed some white powder in half a glass of water. Then she held the glass out to the puppet and spoke to him lovingly.

"Here, my dear boy. Drink this, and in a few days you'll be well again."

Pinocchio stared at the glass, made an awful face, and whined, "Is it bitter or sweet?"

"I'm afraid it's bitter. But it will make you well."

"If it's bitter, then I don't want it!"

"You must drink it! If you do, I'll give you a piece of candy to take away the bitter taste."

"Where's the candy?"

"Right here, dear," said the Blue Fairy, taking a piece from a little golden bowl.

"Let me have my candy first, and then I'll drink your horrible bitter medicine."

"Do you really promise?"

"Yes! Give me the candy!"

The Blue Fairy handed the piece of candy to him, and Pinocchio crunched it between his teeth and swallowed it down instantly. Then he licked his lips and sighed, "Wouldn't it be nice if all candy were medicine? I'd be taking medicine all the time!"

"Now, dear, keep your promise and drink this little bit of water, and soon you'll be all better again."

Pinocchio took the glass, but he was very bad tempered. First he held it away from himself and just poked the tip of his nose into it. Then he brought it closer to his mouth—and poked his nose in again. Then he put it down and said:

"Ugh! It's too bitter! It's too bitter! I can't drink it!"

"How can you say that? You haven't even tasted it yet."

"I know it! I can smell it! First give me another piece of candy—and then I'll drink it."

And the Blue Fairy, with all the patience of a kind mother, put another piece of candy in his mouth. Then, once more, she held out the glass to him.

"No!" said the puppet, making a thousand disgusted faces. "I can't do it!"

"Why not?"

"Because—because that pillow down there near my feet is bothering me."

She took away the pillow.

"No! It's no use! I can't drink it!"

"What's wrong now? Is anything else bothering you?"

"The door of this room bothers me. Why is it half open?"

The Blue Fairy walked over to the door and closed it.

92

"Anyway," screamed Pinocchio, bursting into tears, "this awful medicine-water—I won't drink it! No! No! No!"

"My dear boy, you'll be sorry later if you don't take it."

"I don't care."

"You're very sick."

"I don't care."

"In a few hours your fever will carry you to another world."

"I don't care."

"Aren't you afraid to die?"

"No—not a bit afraid! I'd rather die than drink that disgusting stuff."

Just then the door opened and four rabbits, all coal black, came in. They were carrying a little coffin on their shoulders.

"What is it you want?" screamed Pinocchio, sitting bolt upright in terror.

"We're here for you," said the biggest rabbit.

"For me? But I haven't died yet!"

"No, not yet. But you have only a few more minutes to live, since you won't drink the medicine that can cure your fever."

"Oh, dear, kind Blue Fairy, dear, kind Blue Fairy," shouted the puppet, "please—quickly—hand me that glass! Have mercy! Please hurry! I don't want to die. No, I don't want to die!"

And he seized the glass in both hands and emptied it in one gulp.

"Oh, well," shrugged the rabbits, "this is one trip we didn't need to make!"

And they put the little coffin on their shoulders again

and went away, grumbling and muttering between their teeth.

A few minutes later Pinocchio jumped straight up in the air and out of bed, completely well. For I must tell you: wooden puppets are lucky indeed. They hardly ever get sick; and when they do, they get better at once.

The Blue Fairy watched him running and playing in the room, lively and happy as a young rooster crowing for the

first time, and said, "Then my medicine really cured you?"

"It certainly did! It brought me back into this world."

"Then why in the world did I have all that trouble getting you to drink it?"

"That's how we boys are! We're more afraid of medicine than of being sick."

"Shame on you! You boys ought to know that the right medicine, if you take it in time, can save you from becoming very ill and even dying."

"Yes! Next time I won't be such a nuisance. I'll remember those coal-black rabbits with the coffin on their shoulders and I'll just grab for that medicine and—whoosh!—down it will go!"

"Now, come and sit near me for a moment, and tell me how you happened to meet up with those murderers."

"It happened this way. Fire-eater the puppet master gave me some gold coins and said, 'Here—take these to your papa.' But instead I met a Fox and a Cat—two very fine people—on the road. And they said to me:

" 'Would you like those coins of yours to grow into a thousand coins, and even two thousand? Come with us, and we'll lead you to the Field of Miracles.' And I said, 'Let's go!' And they said, 'Let's stop a while at the Red Crab Inn, and then we'll get going again at midnight.' And when I woke up they weren't there any more, because they had left. Then I began walking in the night—so dark I can't tell you how dark. And I met the two murderers. They had sacks over their heads to disguise themselves, and they said, 'Hand over your money.' And I said, 'I don't have any,' because I had the four gold coins hidden in my mouth. And one of the murderers tried to stick his hand in my mouth and I bit it off in one bite and spat it out. But instead of a hand it was a

cat's paw. And the murderers started chasing me, and I ran toward where you were, until finally they caught me and hanged me by the neck from a tree in these woods and said, 'Tomorrow we'll be back, and you'll be dead by then and your mouth will fall open, and then we'll take those gold coins you're hiding under your tongue.' "

"Where are the coins now?" asked the Blue Fairy.

"I've lost them!" wailed Pinocchio. But that was a lie. He had them in his pocket.

The moment he told the lie, his nose, which was already very long, suddenly grew two fingers longer.

"And where was it you lost them?"

"In the woods, near here."

At this second lie his nose became still longer.

"Nothing to worry about," said the Blue Fairy. "If you lost them in the woods nearby, we'll look for them and find them. We always find anything that's lost in our woods."

"Wait! I'm beginning to remember things better now," said the puppet, who was getting all tangled up in his lies. "I didn't really lose those coins. I swallowed them without thinking when I drank the medicine."

This was the third lie! Pinocchio's nose grew so very long that he couldn't turn around in any direction. If he turned one way, he bumped his nose against the bed and the window panes. If he turned the other way, he banged it against the walls or the door. If he raised his head upward a little, he was in danger of sticking his nose in the Blue Fairy's eye.

She looked straight at him and laughed.

"Why are you laughing?" asked the puppet. He was extremely worried, for his nose by now was quite a sight as well as being so uncomfortable.

"I'm laughing at your lies, dear."

"What makes you think I've been lying?"

"People's lies, my dear, are easy to recognize, because there are only two kinds. Either they're lies with short legs or lies with long noses. Your lies have long noses."

Pinocchio didn't know where to hide, he was so ashamed. He tried to run out of the room, but couldn't. His nose had grown so long he could no longer get through the door.

CHAPTER

A S YOU CAN IMAGINE, THE Blue Fairy let Pinocchio cry and carry on for a good half hour because he couldn't turn around anywhere or even get through the door. She wanted to teach him a good lesson and break his ugly habit of lying, the worst habit a child can have. But when she looked at his face again and saw it all twisted up with misery, with his eyes bulging out of his head, of course she was full of pity. She clapped her hands together, and at this signal a thousand giant woodpeckers flew into the room through the window. They perched on Pinocchio's nose and pecked away at it so furiously that in a few minutes that extravagant monstrosity was back to its normal size.

"How good you are to me, kind Fairy," said the puppet, wiping away the tears from his eyes, "and how much I love you!"

"I love you dearly, too," answered the Fairy. "If you'd

like to stay here with me, you can be my little brother, and I'll always be your sister."

"It would make me very happy to stay with you—but what about my poor papa?"

"Everything has been arranged. I've thought it all over, and your papa has been told that he can be with us too. He's coming tonight. The first thing you know he'll be here, for he's on his way right now!"

"Is he really?" cried Pinocchio, jumping up and down with joy. "Oh, my dear, kind Fairy, if you don't mind I want to go out and meet him. He has suffered so much on account of me, and I want to meet him and kiss him."

"All right, go ahead. But be careful not to get lost. Walk through the woods, and I'm sure you'll meet him pretty soon."

So off Pinocchio went. When he reached the woods he began running like a young deer. But when he reached the Big Oak he stopped. He thought he could hear leaves rustling and people moving about. And sure enough he saw—have you guessed it?—the Fox and the Cat, his two traveling companions, with whom he had dined at the Red Crab Inn.

"Well, look who's here! It's our dear friend Pinocchio!" shouted the Fox, hugging and kissing him. "What brings you here?"

"Yes, what brings you here?" echoed the Cat.

"Oh," said the puppet, "it's a long story. I'll tell you about it when we have more time to relax and talk. But I'll tell you one thing right now, anyway. The other night, after you left me, I met up with murderers on the road."

"Murderers? Oh, you poor Pinocchio! What did they want?"

"They wanted to steal my gold coins."

"Villains!" cried the Fox.

"The worst kind of villains!" cried the Cat.

"But I ran away from them," the puppet continued, "and they ran after me. They kept right behind me and, finally, they caught me and hanged me from the highest branch of the Big Oak over there."

And Pinocchio pointed to the tree, which was just a couple of steps away.

"Did you ever hear of anything worse than that?" said the Fox. "What a world we live in! How can honest people like us feel safe after such a thing?"

While they were talking in this way, Pinocchio noticed that something was wrong with the end of the Cat's right foreleg. The whole paw, with all its claws, was missing! In great surprise, Pinocchio asked, "Whatever happened to your paw?"

The Cat was about to answer, but then grew confused and said nothing. But the Fox spoke up quickly.

"My friend is too modest to tell you. That's why he can't answer, and so I'll answer for him. Just an hour ago we met an old wolf on the road. He was weak with hunger, almost fainting. He begged us for money, or for something, anything, to eat. But we had nothing—not a thing, not even a fishbone. Now what do you think my friend did? He has the great soul of a great man. He's as generous as a king. He bit off his own paw with his own teeth and tossed it to that poor animal to keep him from starving."

As he spoke, the Fox wiped away a tear from his eyes.

Pinocchio, too, was deeply touched. He went up to the cat and whispered in his ear:

"If all cats were like you, wouldn't the mice be lucky!"

"And now tell us," said the Fox. "What brings you to this place again?"

"I've come to meet my papa. He'll be along any minute."

"What about your gold coins? Where are they now?"

"Oh, I keep them in my pocket—all but the one I had to pay at the Red Crab Inn."

"Just think, Pinocchio! Instead of just the four coins, you could make them grow into a thousand—maybe two thousand—by tomorrow! Why won't you take my advice? Come along and plant the money in the Field of Miracles."

"I can't—not today. I'll be glad to come along some other time!"

"Some other time will be too late," said the Fox.

"Why do you say that?"

"Because the Field of Miracles has just been sold. A rich man has bought it, and after tomorrow he won't let people plant money there any more."

"Well, how far away is this Field of Miracles?"

"Not far—just a mile or so. Won't you come with us? In half an hour you can get there, plant the four gold coins at once, and then, a few minutes later, gather up two thousand of them and come back tonight with your pockets full of money. Won't you come?"

Pinocchio hesitated a little before answering. He thought of the kind Blue Fairy and old Geppetto, and he remembered the Talking Cricket's warning. But then he did just what all brainless, heartless children would do. With a little toss of his head he said to the Fox and the Cat:

"All right, then—I'm coming with you!"

And they started out.

After they'd been walking for half the day, they reached

the city called Foolville. Pinocchio noticed at once that the streets were full of dogs whose hair had been shorn off completely and whose mouths were stretched wide open, gaping with hunger. The streets were full, too, of sheep that had also been shorn and were trembling with cold. And there were roosters whose combs and wattles had been cut away and that were begging for even one tiny grain of corn. And there were big, clumsy butterflies that could no longer fly because they had sold their beautiful, colored wings. And there were peacocks without tails that were ashamed to be seen, and pheasants staggering about silently and sadly and mourning for their shining gold and silver feathers, now lost forever.

Amid this throng of poor, disgraced, begging creatures, elegant carriages sometimes drove through. Inside them Pinocchio could see a fox sometimes, or a mean-eyed chattering magpie, or some nasty-looking bird of prey.

"But—where's the Field of Miracles?" he asked.

"Just the tiniest distance more—just over there."

And there it was. They had crossed the city by now and were outside its walls, in a field that, when you looked it over, seemed like any other field.

"At last!" cried the Fox. "Now, Pinocchio, kneel down and scoop up enough dirt to make a little hole, and put your coins in it."

Pinocchio obeyed. He dug the little hole, put his four gold coins in it, and then covered it up again with the dirt he had scooped up.

"Good," said the Fox. "Now go over to that pond over there, fill a pail with water and sprinkle the earth where you've just done your planting."

Pinocchio went to the pond. He didn't have a pail with him, but he took off one of his battered old shoes, filled it with water, and sprinkled the earth just as the Fox had said. Then he asked, "Is there anything more I need to do?"

"No, nothing else," said the Fox. "We must go away now. But you should come back here in about twenty minutes, by yourself. You'll find a young tree already springing up out of the ground, and its branches will be all loaded down with golden coins."

The poor puppet was beside himself with joy. He

thanked the Fox and the Cat a thousand times and promised
to buy them a splendid present.

"Oh, no!" that pair of scoundrels shouted together.
"Thank you very much, but we never accept presents. All
we wanted to do was to show you how to become rich without having to work too hard, and now we're as happy as anyone can be!"

Then they bowed politely, said goodbye to Pinocchio,
wished him a fine harvest of coins, and went their way.

CHAPTER

19

A S THE PUPPET WALKED OFF toward the city, he counted the minutes one by one. The instant he thought it was time, he spun right around and hurried back down the street to the Field of Miracles.

He couldn't wait. He clattered along on racing feet, and his heart was pounding fiercely—*tick-tock, tick-tock*—like a grandfather clock. Meanwhile, he was thinking, "Maybe, instead of a thousand gold coins, I'll find two thousand on the tree! Or maybe I'll find five thousand! What if there are a hundred thousand! I'll be a great lord! I'll have a great palace and a thousand wooden ponies and a thousand separate stables for them, just for the fun of it! I'll have a cellar full of sweet syrups and juices, and a library full of candy and pies and cakes and almond cookies and cream puffs!"

Pinocchio went on dreaming until he came very close to the Field of Miracles. Then he stopped and peered ahead, to spot any tree whose branches might be loaded down with gold coins. But he didn't see any. He went a hundred steps further. Still nothing. Then he reached the field and ran straight to the place where he'd buried his coins. Still nothing. Now he was so worried and puzzled that, forgetting his manners completely, he took his hands out of his pockets and stood scratching his head.

Suddenly he heard a loud burst of laughter. He looked around and saw a huge parrot perched on a tree, preening the few feathers he still had left.

"Why are you laughing?" he asked angrily.

"I'm laughing because I just tickled myself under my wings."

The puppet had no time to answer. He went to the pond, filled his broken-down old shoe with water once more, and again poured water over the earth where his gold coins were buried.

When he did this another burst of laughter, even ruder than the first, rang out over the silent, deserted field.

"All right—out with it!" shouted Pinocchio, losing his temper completely. "Tell me, if you can, you stupid parrot: What do you think you're laughing at?"

"What I'm laughing at is silly people. They believe any nonsense someone tells them, and they let themselves be fooled by anyone who's trickier than they are."

"I suppose you think you mean me?"

"I certainly do, you poor silly Pinocchio. You're so brainless you really think people can sow and reap money like beans and pumpkins. I used to be the same way, and, believe me, I'm paying for it. Now I know (too late!) that to save up a few honest pennies you've either got to work with your own two hands or use your own good brain."

"I don't see what you mean," said the puppet. He was so anxious about his own money by this time that he was trembling with fear.

"Be patient for a moment and you'll see," said the parrot. "In the short time that you were away in the city, the Fox and the Cat came back to this field. They dug up your gold coins and then were off like the wind. Whoever catches them now will have to be pretty smart and work fast!"

Pinocchio stood with his mouth hanging open. He couldn't believe the parrot's words and, with his hands and his nails, began scooping up the earth he had just watered. He kept the dirt flying and made the hole deeper and deeper until you could have put a haystack into it. But the money wasn't there.

Then, completely desperate, he ran all the way back to the city and straight to the courthouse, and reported the two thieves to the judge.

The judge was an ape of the gorilla family. He was a respectable-looking old ape, with a nice white beard and gold-rimmed eyeglasses without lenses. He had to wear glasses all the time, since his eyes had been red and watery for so many years.

Pinocchio stood before the judge and told him the whole story, every single sad little detail, of the cruel trick the Fox and the Cat had played on him. He gave their first and last names and ended by begging for justice.

The judge listened very kindly. He took a sympathetic interest in Pinocchio's story and asked all sorts of questions. You could see how sorry he was for him. Finally, when the puppet had nothing more to say, the judge stretched out his hand and rang a bell.

At this signal two huge dogs—mastiffs—appeared, dressed in policemen's uniforms.

The judge pointed to Pinocchio and said, "This poor

soul has been robbed of his four gold coins. Arrest him at once! March him right off to prison!"

The puppet was thunderstruck. He remained stock still for a moment, and then started to object. But the policemen, to prevent a pointless waste of time, clapped their paws over his mouth and dragged him off to jail.

And there he stayed four whole months—four very long months. He would have had to stay even longer, except for a great stroke of luck. You see, the young Emperor of Folly-land (of which Foolville is the capital) had just won a great war against his enemies. He ordered a splendid public celebration, with colored lights and fireworks and horse races and bicycle races. And, as the most glorious thing of all, he commanded the jailers to unlock the prisons and set all the criminals free.

"If the others are leaving," said Pinocchio to his jailer, "I want to leave too."

"Oh, no," said the jailer, "not you, Pinocchio. You don't belong to the lucky ones I'm supposed to set free. You're not a criminal."

"That's an insult!" cried Pinocchio. "Excuse me, but I happen to be a criminal just like the others!"

"Oh, I beg your pardon," said the jailer. "In that case, you're certainly right." And he took off his hat, bowed respectfully, opened the doors, and let Pinocchio escape, too.

CHAPTER

IMAGINE PINOCCHIO'S JOY! HE was free! Without waiting a single moment, he hurried out of the city and down the road to the Blue Fairy's house.

Because of all the rainy weather, the road had become a muddy swamp. As he went along, Pinocchio sank into the mire again and again—but he didn't mind a bit; for the only thing he wanted was to see his papa again, and his Fairy sister with the blue hair. He bounded along like a greyhound, splashing mud all over himself as he went. And on the way he talked to himself:

"Oh, what bad luck I've been having! It's my own fault, too! I'm a stubborn brat, and I always want everything my own way. I never listen to others, not even to people who want to help me and who know a thousand times more than I do! But from now on I'll be different. I'll be good. I'll be obedient. I've learned my lesson—disobedient children always lose out; they never do anything right. And my papa? Is he still waiting for me? Will he be in the Blue Fairy's house? Poor old man, I haven't seen him for such a long time! I long to hug and kiss him over and over. And the Blue Fairy—will she forgive me? Oh, to think she gave me so much kindness and love, and that it's only because of her that I am still alive! Could there possibly be another boy, anywhere, as ungrateful and heartless as I am?"

Suddenly these thoughts stopped, and so did Pinocchio. He jumped backward four times in horror.

What was it?

Without noticing, he had come right up to a huge, frightful serpent, stretched all the way across the road. Its skin was green, its eyes flashed fire, and the tip of its pointed tail poured forth smoke like a chimneytop.

Can you imagine how frightened that puppet was? He sped to a spot at least a half mile away before he stopped. Then he sat down on a heap of stones, and there he waited for the serpent to go away and leave the road clear again.

He waited an hour. Two hours. Three hours. Still the serpent wouldn't move. Even from a half mile away, Pinocchio could see its fiery red eyes blazing and the column of smoke rising from its tail.

At last Pinocchio decided to be brave. He moved closer to the serpent and spoke to it in a very soft, sweet, and gentle voice:

"I'm terribly sorry, truly, to be bothering you, Mr. Serpent. But I was wondering: Would you please be kind enough to move over just one very tiny bit, just enough to let me pass by?"

He might as well have been talking to a wall. There was no answer.

He tried again, in that same low, sweet, gentle voice:

"I'd like you to know, kind Mr. Serpent, that I happen to be on my way home. My poor papa's waiting for me, and it's been so very long since we last saw each other! Would it be all right, then, please, sir, if I continued on my way?"

He waited for some sign that the serpent had heard and understood him, but no answer came. Instead, the serpent, who until then had seemed so full of life and fire, grew per-

fectly still, almost stiff It closed its eyes, and the smoke stopped rising from its tail.

"What? Can it be true? Is he dead?" cried Pinocchio, rubbing his hands together gleefully. And at once he tried to jump over the serpent and be on his way home again at last. But hardly had he begun his jump when the serpent suddenly shot up to its full height, like a spring that has been released. In a panic, the puppet jerked back, tripped over his own legs, and tumbled to the ground.

He tripped and tumbled so oddly that he did a somersault as he fell and landed upside down, with his head in the mud and his legs sticking up in the air.

At the sight of the puppet in that position, kicking wildly and with his head stuck in the mud, the serpent broke into a fit of laughter. He laughed and laughed and laughed; finally, he laughed so hard he burst a blood vessel in his heart. This time, he really was dead.

After this Pinocchio started running again, for he wanted to reach the Blue Fairy's house before dark. But soon he felt such painful pangs of hunger that he couldn't control himself, and so he jumped into a field near the road to pick a few bunches of the muscatel grapes he saw growing there. If only he hadn't done that!

Hardly had he come near the grapevine when—crack!—he felt his legs gripped by two sharp iron claws. The agony was so piercing that he saw as many stars as there are in the sky.

Our poor puppet was caught in a trap. It had been laid there to catch some big polecats that were raiding all the chicken coops on the neighboring farms.

CHAPTER

21

As you might imagine, Pinocchio began crying and screaming and calling for help. But all his tears and shouts were useless. There were no houses to be seen, and not a living soul passed on the road.

After a while, night came on.

Partly because of the pain caused by the trap, which cut into his shins, and partly because he was afraid to be alone in the dark fields at night, the puppet was about to faint away. Just then, however, he saw a firefly above his head and called out to it.

"Dear little firefly, won't you please help me? Please! Free me from this trap! Oh, it hurts so much!"

"Poor little fellow!" replied the firefly, stopping in the air and beating its wings as it looked at him with pity. "Poor lad! How did you ever let yourself be caught that way, with your legs in that sharp iron trap?"

"I jumped into this field—just to pick some grapes— and—"

"Just a second! Were those grapes yours?"

"No."

"Then who told you it was all right to steal them?"

"I . . . was . . . hungry!"

"Hunger is no excuse, my child."

"I know!" groaned Pinocchio tearfully. "You're right! You're right! I'll never, never do it again!"

Just then they heard the faint sound of approaching footsteps, and they stopped talking. It was the owner of the field, stealing up very softly to see if he had trapped any of the polecats that had been eating his chickens at night.

He came in the dark so that he wouldn't be seen. Imag-

ine his surprise when he suddenly took his lantern out from under his coat and saw a boy in the trap instead of a polecat.

"Aha, you little thief!" he shouted angrily. "So it's you! You're the one that's been stealing my chickens!"

"Not me! Not me!" cried Pinocchio, sobbing. "All I wanted in your field was some of those grapes!"

"People who steal grapes could steal chickens, too. Just you wait, my boy—I'll teach you a lesson you'll never forget!"

And then the farmer opened the trap and grabbed the puppet by the scruff of his neck. He lifted him up and carried him off to his house as easily as he'd have carried a newborn lamb.

When he got to the house, he slammed Pinocchio down to the ground, placed one foot on his neck, and said, "It's getting pretty late and I'm going to bed now. I'll decide about things tomorrow. Meanwhile, since the dog that has been protecting my hens at night died today, I'm giving you his job. From now on, you're my watchdog."

Without another word he slipped a great collar, all covered with brass studs, over Pinocchio's head and tightened it in such a way that the puppet couldn't possibly slip it off without help. A long iron chain, fastened to the wall of the house, was attached to this collar.

"It may rain tonight," said the farmer. "If it does, go lie down in that wooden doghouse. You'll find some straw you can rest on there—the straw my poor dog used as his bed for four years. And if we have bad luck and some thieves come along, remember to prick up your ears and bark."

After telling Pinocchio these things, the farmer went into his house, locking the door behind him. Poor Pinocchio lay shivering on the ground, almost dead with hunger, cold, and fear. Now and then he tugged frantically at the dog collar, which was almost choking him, and whimpered to himself.

"It's my own fault! I certainly deserve it! It's because I'm just a loafer and a drifter, and I've always listened to the wrong people. That's why my luck is always bad. If I'd been good, the way so many little children are, and if I'd really liked to study and work, and if I'd just stayed home with my poor papa, I wouldn't be here now. I wouldn't be lying on the ground at night out in the country somewhere, and I surely wouldn't be forced to work as a farmer's watchdog. Oh, if only I could be born all over again! But it's too late now. I'll just have to wait and be patient."

After he got these thoughts off his chest, he felt a little better. He crawled into the doghouse and fell asleep at once.

CHAPTER

FOR MORE THAN TWO HOURS, Pinocchio slept soundly. But then, toward midnight, he was awakened by faint sounds in the quiet night: first low whispers and then a louder chatter of strange voices. He stuck the tip of his nose out of the dog-house and saw four dark little creatures standing together and talking, as if they were holding a meeting. They looked something like cats but not quite, for they were polecats— animals with a special love for eggs and for young chickens. One of them now came over to the doghouse and said, very softly:

"*S-s-st!* Hello there, Melampo!"

"My name isn't Melampo," answered the puppet.

"No? Then who are you?"

"I'm Pinocchio."

"What are you doing here?"

"It's my job. I'm the watchdog."

"Watchdog? But where's old Melampo? Where's the good old dog who used to be here?"

"He died this morning."

"Oh, what a shame! Poor fellow! He was such a nice dog! But judging by your face, I'd say you were a nice dog, too."

"Excuse me, friend, but I don't happen to be a dog."

"Not a dog? Well, then, what are you?"

"I'm a puppet."

"A puppet! And you're working here as a watchdog?"

"Only too true! It's my punishment."

"Oh, well! Look, we'll make a deal with you—the same one we made with the late, lamented Melampo. He was satisfied with it, and I know you'll be happy, too."

"What kind of deal was that?"

"Simple. The arrangement is this: One night a week we visit this chicken coop and carry out eight chickens. We keep seven to eat ourselves and give one to you. But you must agree to pretend you're asleep all the while and promise never to take it into your head to bark and wake up the farmer."

"So!" said Pinocchio. "Is this the deal you had with Melampo?"

"Exactly. Exactly. And we always got along fine with him. Now you just go back to sleep like a nice doggie. You can be sure that before we leave we'll prepare you a nice plump little chicken, all plucked and ready for your breakfast. Do you get what I'm saying?"

"I get it, all right!" exclaimed Pinocchio, nodding his head in a threatening sort of way as though he were thinking, "I get it—and so will you pretty soon!"

Once the polecats felt safe about Pinocchio, they went right over to the chicken coop. They pulled its little wooden door open with their teeth and claws and slipped in, one behind the other. But the moment the fourth one's tail disappeared, they heard the little door being slammed shut behind them with a violent bang.

It was Pinocchio who had slammed it shut. And to make sure it stayed shut, he also pushed a heavy rock against it.

And then he started barking—*bow-wow, bow-wow, bow-wow*—just as noisily as any watchdog.

When he heard Pinocchio barking, the farmer jumped out of bed, grabbed his rifle, ran to the window, and called down, "Hey! What's going on there!"

"The thieves!" shouted Pinocchio. "I've caught the thieves!"

"Where are they?"

"In the chicken coop!"

"I'm coming!"

And before you could say "Uh," he had already rushed to the chicken coop, seized the four polecats, and tied them up in a sack. He was enormously pleased. He had never felt so triumphant.

"At last!" he said. "At last I've got you. I could punish you myself, but I'm too kindhearted. So tomorrow morning I'll take you into the village and give you to the innkeeper. He'll be glad to skin you and cook you, in a sweet-and-sour sauce, the way he cooks hares. It will be a great honor for you. You don't deserve it, but kindhearted people like me don't make a fuss about little matters like that."

Then he turned to Pinocchio and picked him up and petted him, as if he really were a dog, and asked, "How did you ever figure out the way those little crooks got into my chicken coop? And to think that Melampo, my faithful dear old Melampo, never noticed a thing!"

Now, the puppet could have told him everything he knew. He could have told him all about the dishonest deal between the dog and the polecats. But after all, Melampo was no longer alive, was he? "What's the use," thought Pinocchio, "of telling tales about dead people? The best thing is just to leave them in peace."

And so he said nothing at all about Melampo. And then the farmer asked him another question:

"When the polecats came into the yard, were you awake or asleep?"

"I was asleep," said Pinocchio, "but they woke me up with their chattering. And after a while one of them came to the doghouse and said, 'If you promise not to bark and wake up your master, we'll give you a present of a fine chicken, all plucked and ready to eat. Do you get it, eh?' Imagine anybody's having the nerve to talk to me that way! Because I can tell you this: I may be a puppet who makes lots of mistakes and isn't as good as he should be, but I could never do something like that. I could never steal anything, or accept any gift from somebody who had stolen it."

"You're a good lad!" cried the farmer, patting him on the shoulder. "You have the good heart of an honest person! And to show you how well I think of you, I'm setting you free right now so you can go back home!"

And he knelt down and removed the dog collar from Pinocchio's neck.

CHAPTER

23

THE MOMENT THAT PAIN-
ful, shaming dog collar was
unfastened, Pinocchio started off across the fields. He didn't
stop for a single instant until he reached the road leading to
the Blue Fairy's little house.

Once he reached that road, he stopped to have a good
look all around. The road ran along a high ridge, and down
below he could see the flat plains and, a short distance away,
the woods where he had first had the bad luck to meet the
Fox and the Cat. Among the other, smaller trees, he recognized the top of the Big Oak from which he had been hanged
and left dangling. But, although he looked and looked from
every angle, he couldn't see the little house of the beautiful
blue-haired child at all.

Suddenly a sad feeling gripped Pinocchio's heart.
Something must be wrong! He started running again, with
all the strength he had left in his legs. In a few minutes he
was in the meadow where the little white house had once
stood. But the little white house was no longer there. Instead,
he saw a small marble gravestone with these pitiful words
carved on it:

HERE LIES
THE CHILD WITH THE BLUE HAIR
DEAD BECAUSE OF SORROW
SOON AFTER SHE WAS ABANDONED
BY HER LITTLE BROTHER PINOCCHIO

I leave it to you to imagine how the puppet felt when, somehow or other, he managed to spell out these words. He fell face downward to the ground, and then covered the marble gravestone with a thousand kisses, and burst into a great flood of tears. He cried all night long, and next morning at dawn he was still crying even though his eyes had no tears left. His howls of grief were so piercing and drawn out that they echoed far and wide among the hills.

"O, my dear little Fairy," he lamented, "why did you have to go and die? Why didn't I, who am so bad, die instead of you, who were so good? And my papa, where is he now? O, dear little Fairy, where can I find him? I want to be with him forever and ever! I'll never, never leave him again! O, my little Fairy, tell me it's not true that you're dead! If you really love me, if you love your little brother, come back to life—be the way you were before! Aren't you sorry to see me all alone, with nobody to take care of me? If the murderers come back, they'll hang me from the tree again, and this time I'll really die. Oh, what shall I do? I'm all by myself, and I've lost both you and my papa, and there's nobody to feed me. Where will I sleep at night? Who'll make me a new jacket? Oh, it would have been better, a hundred times better, if I had died too! Yes, I wish I were dead! *Boo-hoo-hoo!*"

In his misery, Pinocchio tried to tear his hair out. But since it was made of wood, he couldn't even have the satisfaction of feeling it between his fingers.

Just then an enormous pigeon, hovering high up in the air on extended wings, called down to him.

"What's the matter, child? What are you doing down there?"

"Can't you see what I'm doing?" said Pinocchio. "I'm crying!" And he lifted his eyes toward the voice from the sky and wiped them with his jacket sleeve.

"Tell me," said the pigeon, "have you ever happened to meet up with a puppet called Pinocchio among your friends?"

"*Pinocchio?* Did you say Pinocchio?" cried the puppet, jumping to his feet. "That's *my* name. *I'm* Pinocchio!"

At once the pigeon flew down to the ground. He was bigger than a turkey.

"You must know Geppetto too, then, I suppose?" he asked.

"Do I *know* him? He's my poor papa! Has he—perhaps—spoken to you about me? Can you take me to him? But . . . but . . . is he still . . . alive? Oh, answer me, please! Tell me! Is he still alive?"

"He was—three days ago. I saw him then, building something on the edge of the sea."

"What was he building?"

"It was a little boat. He wanted to go across the sea in it. That poor man! For more than four months he's been hunting all over the country for you. And since he hasn't been able to find you anywhere, he's decided to look for you far away, in the lands of the New World."

"Is it far from here to the seacoast?" asked Pinocchio.

"More than six hundred miles."

"Six hundred miles! O, my dear Pigeon, how wonderful it would be to have your wings!"

"Do you want a ride? I'll take you there."

"How?"

"Just sit on my back. Are you heavy?"

"Me? Hardly! I'm as light as a leaf."

Then and there, without another word, Pinocchio jumped up astride the pigeon's back, with one leg on each side as if he were on horseback. "Giddyap, little horse!" he shouted happily, "and gallop as fast as you can!"

The pigeon took flight again. In a few minutes they were so high up they almost touched the clouds. Out of curiosity the puppet bent forward a little and looked down. But when he saw how far away the ground was he suddenly was horribly frightened and grew so dizzy that he flung his arms around the pigeon's neck to keep from falling.

They flew all day. Just before dark, the pigeon called out, "I'm thirsty!"

"And I'm hungry!" cried Pinocchio.

"Let's stop there," said the pigeon. "I see a dovecote where we can rest for a few minutes and get some food and water. Then we'll go on, and we should reach the sea by dawn tomorrow."

So they stopped at that deserted dovecote, which had a pan full of water in it and a little basket heaped up with vetch, the green plant doves and pigeons love to eat.

Never in his life had Pinocchio been able to eat vetch. It had always disgusted him and made him sick to his stomach. But that night he gorged himself on it! When he was almost done, he turned toward the pigeon and said, "I would never have believed this stuff could taste so good!"

"Right, my child," answered the pigeon. "When you're really hungry and there's nothing else to eat, even vetch is delicious! Being hungry keeps us from being choosy and silly about what we eat."

After this quick little meal they were ready to leave— and off they flew once more. When morning dawned, they reached the sea.

The pigeon came down and waited until Pinocchio jumped onto the beach. But he shot off again at once into the air, for he did not want the fuss of being thanked for his kindness.

The beach was covered with people. They were shouting and waving and gazing out to sea.

"What's happening?" Pinocchio asked a little old woman.

"What's happening is that an old father, who can't find his little boy anywhere, has made a little boat and is rowing

away to look for him on the other side of the ocean. But today the water's very rough, and that little boat of his is sure to sink."

"Where's the boat right now?"

"Look straight ahead, in the direction of my finger," said the old woman, pointing to something that, far in the distance, seemed to be a nutshell with a tiny man in it.

Pinocchio fixed his eyes on that spot and stared very hard. Then he let out a wild scream and shouted, "That's my papa! That's my papa!"

Meanwhile, the little boat, battered by furious waves, sometimes disappeared among the sea's great, swelling breakers and sometimes could be glimpsed floating beyond them. Pinocchio stood on the top of a cliff and never stopped calling out his father's name and making signals to him with his hands and his handkerchief, and even with his cap.

And it looked as though Geppetto, although he was so far from shore, recognized his little son. For he too waved his cap in the air; and he made gestures to show that he wanted to return, but that the water was too rough for him to use his oars and row back.

Suddenly, without warning, a terrible, vast breaker swamped the boat. It disappeared. The watchers on the shore waited and waited to see it again, but they never did.

"Poor man!" said the fishermen and the other people gathered there. They murmured quiet prayers to themselves, and began moving away toward their homes.

At that moment they heard a desperate wail. They looked back and saw a little fellow standing on a high rock. He dived into the sea, shouting:

"My papa! I'm going to save him!"

Since Pinocchio was made of wood, he kept afloat easily

and could swim like a fish. As he swam, sometimes he disappeared under the powerful waves, and sometimes, very far out, an arm or a leg would flash in the air for a moment. Finally he was completely out of sight.

"Poor kid!" sighed the fishermen and the other people on the shore. And, murmuring quiet prayers to themselves, they began moving away toward their homes.

CHAPTER

T HE THOUGHT OF RESCUING
his poor papa gave Pinoc-
chio the strength to keep swimming all night long.

And what a horrible night! The rain poured in torrents.
It hailed. It thundered. Bolts of lightning made the night
bright as day.

When morning came, Pinocchio could see a long strip of
land before him, not very far away. It was an island in the
middle of the sea.

He kept trying as hard as he could to reach the island,
but it seemed impossible. The huge waves, chasing after one
another and tumbling in every direction, tossed him about
like a twig or a wisp of straw. But at last he had some luck. A
breaker rolled up under him so powerfully and fiercely that
it lifted him high in the air and then flung him violently onto
the sandy shore.

He hit the ground with such a thud that all his ribs and
joints seemed to crack. But Pinocchio comforted himself by
saying, "Ah, well! Once again I've had a narrow escape!"

Meanwhile, little by little, the storm calmed down. The

sky cleared, the sun shone forth brilliantly, and the waves grew still and gentle, as though oil had been spread on them.

The puppet took off his wet clothes to dry them in the sun. Then he looked around in all directions to see if perhaps, on that vast body of water, he might somehow at last manage to catch sight of a little boat with a tiny man in it. But no matter how long and carefully he peered, he saw nothing but the sky and the sea and, once, the sail of some ship so distant it looked like a fly.

"If only I knew the *name* of this island, at least!" he said to himself as he stood on the shore. "And if I could find out whether decent people live here—I mean, people who don't like to hang children from the highest branches of trees! But who can answer these questions for me? Who, since there's no one here?"

The idea that he was completely alone, alone, alone on a great, empty island filled Pinocchio with gloom. In another moment he would have burst into tears. But just then he saw a huge fish moving in the water, quite close to the beach. It was going about its business peacefully, with its head above the water.

The puppet didn't know just how to speak to the fish, for he couldn't tell what kind it was. So he called to it in a loud voice, to make sure it would hear him. "Hi, there, Mr. Fish! May I have a word with you?"

"You may even have two words," replied the fish in a friendly voice. He was a dolphin—so polite you would find only a few others like him if you searched through all the seas of the world.

"Can you tell me . . . do you know . . . if there's some place on this island where I can get something to eat without any danger of being eaten up myself?"

"There certainly is," said the dolphin. "In fact, it's not at all far from here."

"How can I get there?"

"Just take that path over there, to your left. And then follow your nose. You can't miss it."

"Thank you. And now could you please tell me something else? You're always swimming about in the sea, day and night. Haven't you noticed a little boat with my papa in it?"

"And who is your papa?"

"He's the best papa in the world, and I'm the worst son."

"I'm afraid the storm we had last night has sunk his little boat," said the dolphin.

"And my papa?"

"By now the terrible shark, who has been on the war-path lately, and has been causing destruction and misery in our waters, must have swallowed him."

"Is he very big, this shark?" asked Pinocchio, who was trembling with fear.

"*Big?*" said the dolphin. "Maybe you'll get some idea of his size when I tell you he's higher than a five-story building, and his mouth is so wide and deep that a whole railroad train, with its engine burning coal and smoke coming out of it, could easily fit into it."

"*Phew!*" whistled Pinocchio in amazement and terror. He put his clothes back on in a great hurry, looked at the dolphin, and said, "Goodbye, Mr. Fish. Please forgive me for disturbing you, and a thousand thanks for your kindness."

And he started going down the path away from the water at once, walking so fast he seemed to be running. At every little sound he would turn quickly and look behind, shuddering to think he might be followed by the terrible great shark, as high as a five-story building, that could have held a railroad train with its engine pouring forth smoke in its mouth.

In half an hour he reached the little town called Busy-Beeville. Its streets swarmed with people rushing here and there on their errands. Everyone had something to do, and all were working. You couldn't have found an idle person or a tramp, not even if you searched everywhere with a lantern. "Oh, no!" thought that lazy Pinocchio. "I'm afraid this is no place for a fellow like me! I wasn't made for hard work!"

Meanwhile, he began to be frantically hungry. He hadn't eaten a thing, not even a bit of vetch, for more than twenty-four hours.

What to do?

He had two choices: either to find some work or to beg people for a penny or a crust of bread.

He was ashamed to beg. His father had always taught that begging was wrong, except if you're old or sick. When you're really poor you deserve help and sympathy, and those who are too old and sick to earn their bread through the work of their hands do, certainly, have a right to ask for what they need. But the rest of us have the duty to work. If we refuse and therefore suffer from hunger, so much the worse for us.

As Pinocchio stood there thinking, a man came down the street sweating and out of breath. With all his strength, he was pulling two carts loaded with coal behind him as well as he could.

The man had a kind face, Pinocchio thought. And so, with his eyes cast downward in shame, the puppet stepped up to him and quietly said, "I'm almost dead with hunger. Could you please, sir, take pity and let me have just one penny?"

"Just one penny?" repeated the charcoal man. "I'll gladly give you four pennies if you're really that hungry! All you need to do is to help me pull these carts to my house."

Pinocchio felt insulted. "I'm surprised at you!" he said angrily. "I'll have you know I haven't turned into a donkey yet! Don't expect *me* to go dragging carts through the street!"

"Good for you!" answered the charcoal man. "If that's the way you feel, little fellow, and if you're still dying of hunger, just cut yourself two slices of your silly pride to eat and try not to get a bellyache!"

A few more minutes passed, and then a bricklayer came along, carrying a bucket full of lime.

"Would you be good enough, sir, to give a penny to a

poor starving boy, who's so hungry he can't stop yawning?"

"Why not? Just help me carry my lime so I can use it to make some mortar for my bricks, and I'll give you five pennies, not just one."

"But lime is so heavy," said Pinocchio. "I don't want to get myself all tired out."

"Right, my boy! If you don't want to get tired, then just amuse yourself by yawning with hunger. And much good may it do you!"

In less than half an hour, twenty more people passed by. Pinocchio begged them all for help, but they all said something like this:

"Aren't you ashamed of yourself? Instead of loafing about the street, go and find some work to do and learn how to earn your pennies."

Finally a sweet-faced little woman appeared, carrying two large jugs of water.

"Oh, dear kind lady," said Pinocchio, "may I please have a sip of water from one of your jugs?" He was burning with thirst.

"Of course you may, little boy," said the little woman, setting the jugs down on the ground. "Drink your fill, poor lad."

Pinocchio drank like a sponge, and then he wiped his mouth with his hand and whimpered, "I'm not thirsty any more, but I'm so hungry!"

When she heard these words, the little woman smiled gently and said, "If you help me carry one of these water jugs home, I'll give you a big piece of bread."

Pinocchio stared at the jug she was holding out to him, but he didn't say yes or no.

"And with the bread I'll give you a nice plateful of

cauliflower, seasoned with oil and vinegar," the kind woman added.

Pinocchio stared at the jug again, but he still didn't say yes or no.

"And after the cauliflower I'll give you some delicious chocolate candy filled with syrup."

This was too tempting to resist. Pinocchio's mind was made up now, and he said, "Very well, then! I'll carry the water jug to your house."

The jug was very heavy, and the puppet wasn't strong enough to carry it with his hands. He had to balance it on his head.

When they reached her house, the kind little woman invited Pinocchio to sit down at a small table that had already been laid, and she gave him the bread and seasoned cauliflower and the candy.

Pinocchio didn't just eat; he put down his head and gobbled. His stomach felt like a house nobody has lived in for a long time.

Slowly, little by little, his furious pangs of hunger disappeared. At last he raised his head from the plate to thank the lady who had been so good to him. When he did, he let out a long cry of amazement—*oh-h-h-h!*—and sat gaping, with his eyes wide open, his fork in the air, and his mouth full of bread and cauliflower.

"What's the matter, dear child?" laughed the kind lady. "Has something surprised you?"

"It's . . . uh," the puppet stammered, "it's . . . it's . . . because you look like . . . you remind me of . . . yes, yes, yes! . . . the same voice . . . the same eyes . . . the same hair . . . yes, yes, yes! . . . you have blue hair, too . . . like her! Oh, my little Fairy! Oh, my little Fairy! Tell me it's you—you *yourself*! Don't make me cry any more! If you only knew—I've cried so often and suffered so much!"

As he spoke, Pinocchio burst into tears, knelt on the floor, and threw his arms around the knees of that mysterious little woman.

CHAPTER

A T FIRST THE KIND LITTLE woman tried to pretend she wasn't the little blue-haired Fairy. But when it was clear that Pinocchio had recognized her, she stopped making believe and admitted it was so.

"You wicked little puppet," she said. "How in the world did you ever find out?"

"Because I love you so much—that's what told me."

"Do you remember how I used to look? When you went away, I was a little girl. But now I'm a woman, almost old enough to be your mother."

"How happy that makes me! From now on, I won't call you 'little sister' any more. I'll call you 'mama.' For a long time I've longed to have a mama like all the other little boys! But tell me—how did you manage to grow up so quickly?"

"That's a secret!"

"Teach *me* the secret! I want to grow a little bigger, too. Just look at me—don't you see? I'm always the same, no bigger than a crumb of cheese."

"But you can't grow, Pinocchio," the Blue Fairy answered.

"Why not?"

"Because puppets never do grow. They're born puppets, they live as puppets, and they die puppets."

"Oh, but I'm fed up with being a puppet all the time!" he cried, giving himself a sharp rap on his wooden head. "I want to become a man some day, a grown-up person, like everybody else."

"And so you shall, Pinocchio! You will become a man, once you've earned the right to be one."

"No! Will I *really*? Please tell me—how can I earn that right?"

"It's very, very easy. You must just get into the habit of being a nice boy, that's all."

"Oh, then—then you think I'm not one now?"

"Just the opposite, my dear! Nice boys do as they're told. And you, on the other hand—"

"I know. I never do as I'm told."

"And nice boys love to study and work, while you—"

"While I, on the other hand, am lazy and waste time every single day."

"And they always tell the truth."

"And I always tell lies."

"Nice boys are happy to go to school."

"School makes me sick and miserable! But from now on I'm changing my whole life!"

"Do you promise, Pinocchio?"

"I do promise. I want to become a real little boy and make my papa happy. Can you tell me . . . do you know . . . where my poor papa is right now?"

"I'm afraid I don't know."

"Do you think I'll ever, ever be lucky enough to see him again and kiss him?"

"Oh, yes, I do think you will! I'm sure you will!"

At this reply Pinocchio became so joyful that he seized the Blue Fairy's hands and kissed them again and again, with such excitement you'd have thought he was a little crazy. Then, looking up at her lovingly, he asked, "Tell me the truth, little Mama—it wasn't true that you were dead, was it?"

"It seems not," she answered with a smile.

"If you only knew how miserable I was, and how I choked up, when I read those words 'HERE LIES'!"

"I do know. I know very well, and that's why I forgave you. I saw that you could really feel grief, and that you had a true, loving heart. And there's always hope for children with loving hearts, even when they're naughty rascals and have bad habits. There's always hope that they'll take the right path after all. That's why I came here looking for you, you know. I shall always be your own, faithful mama."

"Oh, that's marvelous!" shouted Pinocchio, skipping around the room in a frenzy of delight.

"Will you obey me? Will you always do as I say?"

"Yes! Yes! Yes!"

"Very well, then," said the Blue Fairy. "Starting tomorrow, you'll go to school every morning."

Pinocchio's face fell. He didn't feel like skipping any more.

"And soon you can decide which trade or profession you'd like the best."

Now Pinocchio really looked gloomy.

"What's the trouble?" asked the Blue Fairy, sounding a little irritated. "What is it you're muttering between your teeth?"

"I guess I was thinking," whined the puppet faintly, "that it's a bit too late for me to start going to school."

"No sir! It's never too late to study and learn."

"But I'd hate to have a trade or a profession."

"Why?"

"Because work makes me so tired."

"My dear child," said the Fairy. "Don't you know that people who talk that way end up in jail, or in a hospital? Everyone in the world has to work, you know, whether he or she is rich or poor. Everyone needs to work and feel useful. I pity people with lazy ways! Laziness is an awful disease and has to be cured right away, while you're still a child. Otherwise, it's too late to change, when you become a grown-up."

Somehow these words touched Pinocchio's spirit. He looked up glowingly at the Blue Fairy and cried, "I'll do it! I'll study and work and do exactly as you say! I'm sick of the life of a puppet. I want to be a human boy, no matter what I have to do. You really did promise me that, didn't you?"

"Yes, my dear, it's true. I did promise. But now it all depends on you."

CHAPTER

26

THE NEXT DAY PINOCCHIO went to school.

Imagine how those mischievous boys behaved when they saw a puppet come into their school! They burst out laughing, and they never stopped laughing and playing their silly tricks on him. One boy would snatch his cap. Another would pull at his jacket from behind. Another would try to draw a mustache under his nose with ink. One boy was even bold enough to try to attach strings to his hands and feet, to make him dance.

For a little while Pinocchio stayed calm and went his own way. But finally, one day, he lost patience and turned on the boys who were pestering him and teasing him the most. He gave them a warning look and said, "Watch out, you kids! I didn't come here to have you make fun of me! I'm treating you with respect, and you'd better treat me the same way!"

"Hooray!" shouted one of his tormentors. "Hooray for you, wise guy! You sound like something printed in a book!" And they all howled with wild glee. One of them, the boldest of the lot, reached out his hand to tweak the puppet's nose.

But he didn't move fast enough. Pinocchio stretched his leg out under a table and gave him a good, hard kick in the shins.

"Ow!" howled the boy, rubbing his bruises. "He's got hard feet!"

"And hard elbows! They're even worse than his feet!" cried another boy, whose crude tricks had just earned him a sharp jab in the stomach.

After that kick and that elbow jab, Pinocchio had the respect and sympathy of all the boys at school. From that time on they were kind and friendly, and acted as though they were all his pals.

The teacher thought well of him, too. Pinocchio paid attention, studied all his lessons, was bright and alert, and was always the first pupil to arrive in the morning and the last to leave at the end of the day.

He had only one fault. He made friends with too many of his classmates, including a number of pretty nasty fellows best known because they had no wish to study or do themselves credit in any way.

Pinocchio's teacher warned him about all this every day. The kind Fairy, too, warned him and often repeated, "Be careful, Pinocchio! Those worthless classmates of yours will get you to stop loving your studies one of these days. And maybe they'll get you to do something you'll regret."

"No danger of that!" answered the puppet, shrugging his shoulders and pointing at his forehead as if to say, "I've got too many brains in here to let that happen."

But one fine day, while he was walking to school, he happened to meet up with a bunch of his brand-new pals. They ran up and said, "Have you heard the latest news?"

"No."

"A great big shark, big as a mountain, has appeared in the sea, down near the beach."

"Is that really true? I wonder if it could possibly be the same shark that was there when my poor papa drowned."

"Well, we're going down to the beach to see him. Come along with us."

"Not me, thanks. I'm on my way to school."

"School? What does that matter? We can go to school tomorrow. Whether we're there one day more or one day less, we'll still be the same old donkeys as always."

"But what will the teacher say?"

"He can say whatever he likes. He gets paid to grumble all day long anyway."

"And what about my mama?"

"Mamas never know anything!" sneered all the little wretches together.

"Do you know what?" asked Pinocchio. "I do want to see the shark, for my own reasons. But I'll go over to the beach after school."

"You poor idiot," cried one of the boys. "Why should a fish that size wait for you to come when you're good and ready? As soon as he's bored he'll move on somewhere else, and that'll be the end of that."

"How far is the beach from here?" asked the puppet.

"Not very far. We can be there and get back in less than an hour."

"All right, let's go!" shouted Pinocchio. "The first to get there is champion!"

At this, the whole gang dashed off across the fields with their books and notebooks under their arms. Pinocchio was always ahead of the others. He seemed to have wings on his feet. Every so often he looked back to sneer at his pals, who remained quite a way behind him. When he saw them exhausted and panting for breath, with their tongues hanging out and their hair and clothes covered with dust, he couldn't help laughing with all his heart. Poor little fellow! At that moment he could hardly guess the horrors and the terrible misfortunes toward which he was running so fast.

CHAPTER

27

WHEN HE REACHED THE SEA, Pinocchio looked intently out over the water, in every direction. But there was no shark anywhere in sight. The surface was perfectly smooth, like an enormous crystal mirror.

"Huh!" he snorted, turning to his classmates. "Where's that so-called shark of yours?"

"Maybe he's gone home to make himself breakfast," one boy answered, snickering.

"Or maybe he decided to lie down in his bed for a short nap," added another, with a loud horselaugh.

These stupid, sarcastic answers, and the boys' silly guffaws, showed Pinocchio what a mean joke they had played on him. They had led him to believe something they knew wasn't true. In his anger he spoke to them sharply.

"And now what? What good did it do you to make up your little story about the shark? What was the point?"

"Oh, it was a lot of fun!" shouted the tricksters, talking in a chorus.

"But why?"

"It was a lot of fun to make you miss school and come here with us! Aren't you ashamed to be such a sissy, always on time, always doing your homework? Such a good little boy! Aren't you disgusted with yourself for studying so hard all the time?"

"What if I do study? What makes you think that's any business of yours?"

"It certainly is our business. Because of you, the teacher thinks everybody else in the class is a fool."

"Why's that?"

"Because pupils like you, who always study, make the rest of us, who never want to study, look bad, that's why! And we don't want the teacher to think we're stupid! We have our pride too, you know!"

"Then what am I supposed to do, to make you happy?"

"You've got to be like us. You've got to hate school, and your lessons, and the teacher: our three great enemies."

"But what if I don't hate them? What if I want to go on being a good student?"

"In that case you're not our friend any more. We won't have anything to do with you. And the first chance we get, we'll make you pay dearly—just you wait!"

"That's ridiculous. You make me laugh!" said the puppet, with a shrug and a toss of his head.

"Hey, you dumb Pinocchio," yelled one of the bigger boys, thrusting his face right into the puppet's, "you better not try any show-off tricks with us! Don't come around us crowing like a rooster! Because if you're not afraid of us, we're not afraid of you, either. There's only one of you, and there are seven of us!"

"Sure, *seven*—like the seven deadly sins," said Pinocchio with a defiant laugh.

"Did you hear what he said? He's insulting us all! He called us the seven deadly sins!"

"Better apologize, Pinocchio! If you don't, you're in trouble!"

"You're cuckoo!" jeered the puppet, thumbing his nose at the whole gang in front of him.

"You'll be sorry, Pinocchio!"

"Cuckoo!"

"We'll beat you like a donkey!"

"Cuckoo!"

"You'll go home with your nose in splinters!"

"Cuckoo!"

"I'll teach you to say 'Cuckoo'!" shouted the toughest boy of all. "Take this, meanwhile, for a start, and eat it for your supper tonight!"

And he brought his fist down on Pinocchio's head.

Pinocchio, as you'd expect, returned blow for blow. He fought back, he moved about quickly and jumped here and there, and soon was in a hot battle with the whole gang.

Although he stood alone against them all, Pinocchio defended himself like a hero. And he used those very hard wooden feet of his, too; he used them so well that his enemies kept at a respectful distance. Whenever those feet got near enough to someone to kick him, they left a painful bruise as a souvenir.

Then the boys, furious because they couldn't match blows with a little puppet in a fair fight, got the idea of throwing things instead. They opened their schoolbags and began flinging books at him: spelling books, grammar books, dictionaries, books of stories, and all their other books. But our clever puppet had quick, sharp eyes. He dodged them all skillfully, and the books went flying over his head and into the sea.

Well, imagine how all the fish in the water felt! They naturally supposed the books were some kind of food, and they swam up in great shoals to the top of the water. But once they nibbled on a page or two, or a frontispiece, they quickly spat it out with a disgusted expression, as if to say, "Ugh! This isn't our kind of food! We're used to something a lot better!"

Meanwhile, the battle grew fiercer. Finally, a huge crab, who had left the water and crawled his way very, very slowly up the beach, boomed out in a deep, hoarse voice that sounded like a trombone with a cold:

"Stop it, you idiotic little dumbbells! That's all you really are! Don't you know that this kind of gang fighting between boys always ends badly? Something awful always happens!"

Poor old crab! He might as well have tried to argue with the wind! Even Pinocchio turned nasty for a second. He whirled around, gave the crab a threatening look, and snarled, "Shut up, you stupid, tiresome crab! Why don't you take a couple of cough drops for that ugly croak in your dumb throat? Or better still, go to bed and work up a sweat to cure it!"

Just then the boys, who had by now thrown all their

own books away, noticed the puppet's schoolbag lying on the sand. They grabbed hold of it before he had time to stop them.

Among the books inside was one bound in heavy covers, with a leather spine and strong leather corners. It was called *The Complete Study of Every Kind of Arithmetic*. I leave it to you to decide whether or not it was a thick book that weighed quite a lot!

One thoughtless boy snatched up this book, aimed it at Pinocchio's head, and threw it with all his might. But he missed the puppet and hit one of his own friends in the head instead. The lad sank to the ground, turned as white as a newly starched sheet, and said these six words:

"Oh, Mama, help me! I'm dying!"

Then he lay silent, stretched out on the sand of the beach.

At sight of the dead boy, his frightened friends ran off at once. In a few moments they were all out of sight.

But Pinocchio didn't run away. Full of grief and afraid, he himself felt more dead than alive. And yet he ran down to the sea and soaked his handkerchief in the water, and then came back and began to bathe his poor schoolmate's temples. And as he did so he cried desperately and kept calling the boy's name and talking to him:

"Oh, poor Eugenio! Open your eyes and look at me! Why don't you answer me? Please believe me, Eugenio, it wasn't me that did it! Open your eyes! If you keep them closed, I'll die too! Oh, dear God, how can I ever get up the courage to go back home after this, to my kind mama? What will become of me? Where can I go? Where can I hide? Oh, how much better off I'd be if I'd gone to school this morn-ing—a thousand times better off! Why did I ever listen to those fools? Now they've ruined my life! My teacher told me, and my mama repeated: 'Stay away from bad companions!' But not me! I'm too stubborn and willful! I hear people talking to me, but I don't really listen. So I do things my own way, and then I have to pay for it. That's why I've never been happy for even fifteen minutes since the day I was born. Oh, lord, what's to become of me? What's to become of me? What's to become of me?"

And he continued to cry and sob and punch himself on the head and call on poor Eugenio by name. Then, suddenly, he heard the low sound of approaching footsteps.

He turned and looked up. Two policemen stood there.

"What's going on? What are you doing there on the ground?" they demanded.

"I'm looking after my classmate here."

"Is something wrong with him?"

"It certainly looks like it!"

"Indeed there *is* something wrong with him!" shouted one of the policemen, stooping down and examining Eugenio closely. "This boy has been wounded in the temple! Who did it?"

"Not me!" stammered the puppet, who hardly had any breath left after all his fighting and sobbing.

"Who did it, then?"

"Not me."

"What caused the wound?"

"This book."

And the puppet picked up *The Complete Study of Every Kind of Arithmetic*, with its thick covers made of heavy cardboard and leather, to show it to the policemen.

"Who's the owner of this book?"

"I am."

"That's all we wanted to know. No other information is needed. Come on, now—get up and go along with us."

"But I—"

"Just come along!"

"I'm innocent!"

"Just come along!"

Before leaving, the policemen called out to some fishermen who happened to be going by in their boat, and said, "We charge you to look after this boy who has been wounded in the head. Take him home with you and look after him. We'll be back to check on him tomorrow."

After this they made Pinocchio stand between them and ordered him to march like a soldier.

"Forward, march! And you'd better march on the double, or you'll regret it!"

Without asking them to repeat the command, the puppet started marching very fast along the path leading to the village. But the poor wretch hardly knew where in the world he was. He seemed to be in a dream—and what a hideous dream! He wasn't himself at all. His eyes saw double, his legs shook, his tongue stuck to the roof of his mouth, and he couldn't speak a single word. And yet, in that state of shock, he felt a pain within as though a sharp thorn were piercing his heart. It was the thought of being taken by the policemen past his kind, dear Fairy's window. He would rather, by far, have been dead!

They had already reached the village and were about to enter it when a gust of wind blew Pinocchio's cap off and carried it about ten yards away.

"If you don't mind," said the puppet to the policemen, "I'd very much like to go and pick up my cap."

"All right, but make it snappy!"

The puppet darted over and picked up the cap. But instead of putting it back on his head he stuck it in his mouth between his teeth and shot away toward the beach like a bullet out of a rifle.

The policemen decided they couldn't catch him themselves, and so they set loose their giant police dog, a mastiff that had won first prize in all the world's dog races, to chase him. We know what a good runner Pinocchio was, but the dog was even faster. All the townspeople crowded to their windows and packed the streets, eager to see how this terrifically fierce race would end. But they were disappointed. Pinocchio and the mastiff kicked up so much dust along the way that after a few minutes nobody could see a thing.

CHAPTER

DURING THIS DESPERATE chase there was one terrible moment when Pinocchio was sure the end had come. They had been running and running, as you know, and Alidoro (that was the mastiff's name) had come so close he could almost have swallowed him.

The puppet heard the heavy panting of that frightful animal just the tiniest space behind him, and felt the dog's hot breath on the back of his neck!

Luckily, they were very close to the beach now. The sea was just a few yards off.

The moment he touched the beach the puppet made a tremendous leap, just as good as any frog's, all the way into the water. Alidoro tried to stop himself, but he was going too fast. He hurtled far out, into deep water. The miserable creature didn't know how to swim. He made clumsy movements with his paws, hoping to keep his head above the surface, but the more he struggled the further down he sank.

Then he rose to the surface again. Poor Alidoro! His eyes were rolling in panic, and he was screaming:

"Help! I'm drowning! I'm drowning!"

"Good!" shouted Pinocchio from a distance, safe now from any danger.

"Oh, help me, my dear little Pinocchio! I'm going to die!"

At this cry of anguish the puppet, who was really very goodhearted, felt a wave of pity. He looked straight into the dog's eyes and said, "Well, now! If I do save you, do you promise to leave me alone and never chase me again?"

"I do! I do! But hurry! Have pity! Another few seconds and I'll be dead!"

Pinocchio hesitated for an instant. Then he remembered something his papa had often told him: "A kind deed is always worth doing." He swam over to Alidoro, grasped his tail with both hands, and steered him, safe and sound, onto the dry sand of the beach.

The poor dog couldn't stay on his feet. Without wishing to, he had swallowed so much salt water that he was swollen like a balloon. Still, the puppet was afraid to trust him completely and decided it would be wise to jump back into the sea. He swam out quite a distance, and then he shouted a farewell to the friend he had just rescued.

"So long, Alidoro! Have a nice trip back home and give everybody my regards!"

"So long, Pinocchio!" answered the dog. "A thousand thanks for what you've done! You saved me from death—it was a very great kindness! And you know that, in this world of ours, one good turn deserves another. Some day, if we ever have a chance, we'll talk about all this again!"

Pinocchio went on swimming, keeping close to the shore. At last he thought he had come to a safe place to leave the water. He looked the beach over carefully and caught sight of something on top of a little rocky hill that looked like a cave. A long stream of smoke was rising from it.

"There must be a fire burning in that cave," he thought. "Fine! I can dry off in there and get warm. But what then? Well, I'll find out when it happens!"

His mind was made up. He swam toward the cliffs further down the beach. But just as he was about to leave the water, he felt something pushing him from underneath, raising him higher and higher and higher into the air. He tried to get away, but it was too late—and, to his amazement, he found himself trapped in a great net, together with a swarm of fish of every size and shape, all wriggling and thrashing about vainly like so many lost souls.

At the same time, he saw the fisherman who had caught him coming out of the cave. The man was so ugly, so unbelievably ugly, that surely he was some kind of sea monster. Instead of hair on his head, he had a thick, bushy clump of green grass. His skin was green, his eyes were green, and his long flowing beard, which reached the ground, was green. At first sight, he looked like a gigantic green lizard standing up on its hind legs.

The fisherman pulled the net out of the sea and began shouting aloud with happiness:

"Glorious! Thank heaven! Again today! More fish! Once again I'm going to have a marvelous fish dinner!"

"Lucky for me I'm not a fish!" Pinocchio thought, picking up a bit of courage again.

The green man lifted the net, with all its struggling fish (and Pinocchio), and carried it into his dark and smoky cave, in the middle of which a frying pan full of oil was sizzling away. The greasy smell was so strong you could hardly breathe.

"Now!" cried the green fisherman. "Now we'll see all the kinds of fish I've caught today!" And he thrust one of his oddly shaped hands, which resembled the great shovels bakers use to take the bread out of their ovens, into the net and pulled out a squirming mass of red mullet.

"*Mmmm!* What splendid red mullet!" he cried, gazing at them and smelling them proudly. When he was through smelling them, he tossed them into a huge tub that had no water in it.

And he did the same thing with every handful of fish he pulled out of the net, again and again. Each time the sight of them made his mouth water, and he would laugh and sing out:

"Oh, what splendid whiting!"

"Oh, what exquisite gray mullet!"

"What delicious sole!"

"What marvelous sea bass!"

"What dear little anchovies, with their tiny heads still attached!"

And each time, of course, the whiting, or the sole, or the gray mullet, or the sea bass, or the anchovies went flying into that huge tub to join the red mullet.

At last only Pinocchio remained in the net.

When the green fisherman reached all the way down and pulled him out, his vast green eyes opened wide in shocked surprise. In a startled voice, he bellowed, "What's this? What kind of fish can it be? I can't ever remember seeing or eating a fish made this way!"

He stared and stared, studying the puppet from every angle. Finally he exclaimed, "Of course! I see now! It must be a deep-sea crab!"

Pinocchio's feelings were hurt. To think of mistaking him for a crab! He spoke up indignantly.

"How dare you call me a crab! Just be careful how you talk about me! I'll have you know—with your kind permission—that I'm a puppet!"

"A puppet?" said the fisherman. "To tell you the truth, that's a new one on me. I've never heard of a *puppetfish* before! But so much the better—I look forward all the more to eating you. I can't wait to find out how you taste!"

"*Eating* me?" cried the puppet. "Look at me. Can't you see I'm not a fish? Don't you hear me talking and reasoning, just like you?"

"You're right," said the fisherman. "I have to admit it. And since I do see that you're a fish who happens to be able to talk and reason, like me, I'm going to treat you with the respect you deserve."

"Oh, fine! But would you please tell me just what you mean by that?"

"Well, to show my friendship and pay special honor to you, I'm going to let you choose the way you'd like me to cook you. Would you rather be fried, or would you prefer to be stewed in tomato sauce?"

"I'll be honest with you," said Pinocchio. "What I'd like most, if it's really up to me, is for you to set me free and let me go home."

"You must be joking! You don't want me to miss the chance to taste such a rare fish, do you? It's not every day that someone catches a puppetfish in these waters! But look—don't worry! I'll take good care of you, all right. I'll fry you in my own pan, with all the other fish, and you'll have a great time. It always feels better to be fried in good company."

When he heard this little speech, Pinocchio began crying and screaming and pleading.

"How much better off I'd be," he sobbed, "if I'd gone to school this morning. I was wrong to go along with my classmates, and now I'm paying for it. *Boo-hoo!*"

And he wriggled and jumped like an eel, and tried to slither out of the green fisherman's grip. He struggled so hard that the fisherman plucked some long reeds growing nearby, bound him hand and foot in them, like a sausage, and then tossed him into the tub with all the fish.

Then the fisherman took a great wooden bowl full of flour and began rolling the fish in it. As soon as each fish was covered with flour, he threw it into the hot frying pan.

The first to dance in the sizzling oil were the poor whiting. Then came the sea bass, then the mullets, then the sole, then the anchovies—and then it was Pinocchio's turn! Seeing himself so close to death (and what a dreadful death!) terrified him and made him tremble so much that he had neither voice nor breath left to plead any longer.

And yet our poor little friend did plead—with his eyes! Unfortunately, though, the green fisherman didn't even glance at him. He simply rolled him in the flour five or six times, covering him so completely from top to bottom that he looked like a puppet carved out of chalk.

Then he grabbed Pinocchio by the head and . . .

CHAPTER

ND JUST THEN, AS THE
fisherman was about to toss
Pinocchio into the frying pan, a giant dog came charging into
the cave, drawn by the exciting, mouth-watering smell of
frying.

"Get out!" roared the fisherman, shaking his fist at the
dog and keeping a tight grip on the flour-covered puppet.

But the poor animal was hungry enough for four giant
dogs. He howled and wagged his tail at the same time, as if to
say, "Oh, please! Give me one or two bits of fish, and then I'll
go away quietly."

"Get out, I tell you!" the fisherman repeated. And he
lifted his leg far back, getting ready to give the dog a tremendous kick.

Now this was a dog who, when he was really hungry,
had a terrible temper; he wouldn't even have let a fly rest on
his nose for a moment without blowing up with fury. Nothing could stand in his way. And so, when the green man got
ready to kick him, the dog snarled wildly and showed his
great, pointy fangs.

At that moment he heard a faint little voice calling to him:

"Alidoro! Save me, Alidoro! If you don't, I'll be fried! I'll be done for!"

The dog recognized that voice at once. To his great surprise, he saw that it was coming from an odd, flour-covered bundle in the fisherman's hand.

And what do you think he did? He made a sudden jump from the ground, snatched that flour-covered bundle in his jaws, and then—holding it ever so gently between his teeth—charged back out of the cave and was away, quick as a lightning flash.

The fisherman was enraged. What a disappointment, to have a fish he'd been so eager to eat snatched right out of his hand! He started to chase the dog, but after only a few steps he had a coughing fit and had to quit and go back.

Meanwhile, Alidoro reached the path that led into the village. He stopped running and, very delicately, placed his friend Pinocchio on the ground.

"I owe you so much!" said the puppet. "How can I ever thank you enough?"

"No need to thank me," said the dog. "You saved me not long ago, and one good turn deserves another. That's the way things are—we all have to help each other in this world!"

"But how did you happen to find your way into that cave?"

"Easy. I was still lying there, stretched out on the beach and more dead than alive, when the wind carried the smell of frying fish to me. The smell stirred my appetite, and I got up and followed it. If I'd arrived only a minute later—"

"Don't speak of it!" howled Pinocchio, still trembling with fear. "Don't ever mention it to me! If you had arrived only a minute later, by now I'd have been fried, eaten, and digested. *Brrr!* It gives me the shivers just to think about it!"

Alidoro laughed and held out his right paw to the puppet, who shook it heartily to show his strong friendship. Then they parted, each to go his own way.

The dog went off toward his home. Pinocchio, on his own again, noticed a little cabin not far off and went over to it. An old man sat in the doorway, warming himself in the sun.

"Tell me, good sir," said Pinocchio to the old man, "do you happen to know anything about a poor young lad named Eugenio—a boy whose head was wounded?"

"Oh, yes! Some fishermen brought him to this very cabin, and now—"

"—and now he must be—dead!" Pinocchio broke in, shaking his head sadly.

"No! He's alive! He's already gone back home."

"Alive? Alive?" cried Pinocchio, bouncing up and down with joy. "Really? Then his wound wasn't serious?"

"No, it wasn't. But it might have been very, very serious. He might even have died," said the old man. "Somebody threw a very heavy book, with a hard binding, right at his head."

"Do you know who that was?"

"A classmate of his—a certain Pinocchio."

"Pinocchio?" said the puppet, pretending not to know the name. "And who is this Pinocchio?"

"Not a very nice boy, I should imagine. They say he's a reckless fellow—a pest and a troublemaker."

"Lies! Those are all lies!"

"Oh, then—so you do know this fellow Pinocchio?"

"Certainly—though only by sight!"

"And what do *you* think of him?"

"A fine boy, from all I've heard. He loves his studies, and he's obedient, and he's very kind to his papa and his family."

The puppet was having a good time stringing out these barefaced lies, when suddenly he happened to touch his nose. It had grown four or five inches longer! He shook with fright and shouted, "No! No! Don't believe these things I'm saying, dear sir! I do know this Pinocchio very well, and I can assure you he's a disagreeable young scamp. He's disobedient and he's lazy, and instead of going to school he hangs around the streets with his friends and does nothing but make trouble."

The moment he finished blurting out these words, his nose shrank back to its natural size.

"But what about you?" said the kindly old man. "How did you get to be completely white, from top to toe?"

"I—I'll tell you. I brushed against a wall that had just been whitewashed, without noticing it until it was too late," said the puppet. He felt too embarrassed to confess he had been rolled in flour, like a fish, to be fried in a pan.

"And what about your clothes? Where's your jacket? Where's your cap? What happened to your pants?"

"I met some robbers on the road, and they took them all away from me. Will you help me, please, kind sir? Do you have some old clothes in your house, some things you don't need, that you could give me so I can go home in them?"

"My poor boy! The only useful thing I can give you is my little cloth sack that I keep beans in. If you'd like to have it, please take it! There it is, just over there."

Pinocchio didn't wait to be offered the sack again. He picked it up at once and, with a pair of scissors, cut a hole in the bottom and two smaller holes on each side. Then he pulled the sack over his head and put his arms through it. It covered him like a long shirt. And now that he was at least partly dressed, he started off once more for the village.

But as he walked along he felt uneasy. He felt so uneasy that he would take one step forward and then another step backward, over and over, talking to himself all the while:

"How will I ever face my kind little Fairy again? What will she say when she sees me? Will she forgive my bad behavior a second time? I can't believe it! Oh, no, certainly she won't! And it serves me right, because I'm no good. I'm not to be trusted. I keep promising to change, but I never do change."

It was late at night when he reached the village, in the midst of a storm. The rain was pouring down and it was pitch black, and so Pinocchio ran straight to the Fairy's house. In spite of all his doubts he had made up his mind to knock at the door and walk right in.

When he actually reached the door, however, he lost his nerve. Instead of knocking, he ran back about twenty yards or so and waited. Then he went up to the door a second time, but stood there, undecided. So away he went again—a short distance—and after that he tried for a third time. And once again, he couldn't bring himself to knock. The fourth time, though, he tremblingly took hold of the iron door-knocker and touched the door with it, very lightly.

Now he waited, and waited, until, finally, after half an hour, a top-floor window opened. (It was a four-story house.) A rather large snail, with a lamp glowing on her head, appeared at the window and asked, "Who can you be, at this hour?"

"Is the Fairy home?" asked the puppet.

"The Fairy's asleep. She doesn't wish to be disturbed. But who are you to ask?"

"I'm me!"

"Who's 'me'?"

"Me! Pinocchio!"

"Pinocchio? Who's that?"

"The puppet who lives in this house, with the Blue Fairy."

"Oh," said the snail. "I see. Wait right there for me. I'm coming down to let you in."

"Do hurry up! Have pity on me, please—I'm freezing to death!"

"My dear boy, I'm a snail! We snails never hurry."

An hour passed. Two hours. But the door never opened. By this time Pinocchio, soaking wet and shivering with cold and fear, made up his mind to knock again, this time a little louder.

At this second knock, a window opened on the third floor. The same snail looked out.

"Come on, dear slow little snail," shouted Pinocchio. "I've been waiting for two hours! And two hours, on a night like this, feels longer than two years. Hurry, please, out of pity for me!"

"My dear boy," answered that slow, calm little creature, "I'm a snail, and we snails never hurry!"

And she closed the window.

A short time later, the village clock struck midnight. Then it struck one o'clock in the morning. Then, two o'clock. And the door was still closed.

Then Pinocchio lost his temper. He was in a fury. He seized the knocker, meaning to bang it against the door so hard the whole house would shake with the noise. But the iron knocker suddenly became a live eel. It slithered out of his hands and disappeared into the little stream of rainwater that was now gushing down the middle of the street.

"All right, then!" yelled Pinocchio, absolutely blind with rage by now. "If the knocker can decide to change into an eel and disappear, I guess I can decide to kick the door in!"

And with that he stepped back and let go a mighty kick against the door. The kick was so powerful that his foot went halfway through the wood and then stuck there. The puppet tried to pull it back out, but it was no use trying. His foot remained firmly stuck in the wood, like a well-hammered nail.

Poor Pinocchio! Just picture it! He had to spend the rest

of the night with one foot on the ground and the other one up in the door.

The next morning, as the sun was just beginning to rise in the sky, the door finally opened. That wonderful, dear creature, the snail, had taken only nine hours to come down three flights of stairs to the door. She must really have been sweating after all that exercise!

"What in the world are you doing with your foot stuck in the door?" she asked, laughing.

"I had a silly accident. Sweet, beautiful little snail, won't you kindly see if you can help me out of this torture?"

"My dear boy, you need a carpenter for a job like that. I never claimed to be a carpenter!"

"I beg you! Please! Won't you be good enough to ask the Fairy to help me?"

"The Fairy's asleep. She doesn't wish to be disturbed."

"But what do you expect me to do all day, stuck in the door this way?"

"Try counting all the ants marching up and down the street!"

"Well, anyway, would you at least bring me something to eat? I'm weak with hunger."

"Right away!" said the snail.

And three and a half hours later, she really did come back to Pinocchio with a silver tray on her head. On the tray were a loaf of bread, a roasted chicken, and four ripe apricots.

"Here's your breakfast," said the snail. "The Fairy herself told me to bring it to you."

At this sign of heavenly kindness, the puppet felt happy again. But imagine his disappointment a moment later, when he discovered that the bread was made of plaster, the chicken

of cardboard, and the four apricots of alabaster, painted to look like natural fruit!

He wanted to cry. He wanted to give up in despair. He wanted to throw the tray, and everything on it, at somebody. But instead, either because he was so unhappy or because he was so weak with hunger, he fainted and hung there, with his foot still in the door.

When he came to, later, he was lying on a sofa, with the Blue Fairy sitting beside him.

"I'm going to forgive you, Pinocchio," she said, "just one more time. But if you make any more trouble for me, woe to you!"

Pinocchio swore that he would always study and behave well from that time on. And, for the rest of the year, he did keep his word. In fact, he did better than anyone else in the school when he took his final examinations. His behavior, too, was so pleasing and so good generally that one day the Fairy made a gleeful announcement.

"Tomorrow, at last, your great wish will come true!"

"My great wish? What do you mean?"

"Tomorrow you'll stop being a wooden puppet and you'll turn into a fine, real boy!"

Unless you'd seen him then and there, you'd never be able to guess Pinocchio's delight at this news he'd waited to hear for such a long time. All his friends and schoolmates had to be invited next morning to a very grand breakfast, so they could all celebrate the happy event together. The Fairy prepared two hundred cups of coffee-with-milk, and four hundred rolls that were buttered on *both* sides! It was going to be a marvelous day, a lovely day, but . . .

Unfortunately, in the life of a puppet, there's always a *but* that spoils everything.

CHAPTER

30

OF COURSE, PINOCCHIO ASKED the Blue Fairy's permission to go through the village inviting his friends to the grand breakfast the next morning. The Fairy agreed.

"Yes, certainly. You should go around and invite your friends! But remember: Come back home before it gets dark. Is that clear?"

"Yes!" answered the puppet. "I promise you I'll be back in less than an hour."

"Make sure of it, Pinocchio! Children make promises easily, but too often they forget them."

"But you know I'm not like other children. When I say something, I really mean it."

"Hmm—well, we'll see. If you disobey me this time, you'll be sorry!"

"Why?"

"Because children who don't listen to grown-ups who know more than they do always get themselves into trouble and have a great deal of misery."

"That's something I've learned, all right!" said Pinocchio. "I'll never make that kind of mistake again!"

"We'll see if you're right, my dear."

And so the puppet kissed her goodbye—the good, kind Fairy, who was the closest thing to a mama he'd ever had. Then he went singing and skipping out of the house.

In less than an hour he had invited all his friends. Some of them accepted enthusiastically, at once. Others had to be coaxed a bit at first, but when they heard about the rolls that would be buttered on *both* sides, and the coffee-with-milk, they all ended by saying the same thing:

"Yes, I'll be happy to accept—just to please you!"

Now, among Pinocchio's friends and classmates was one boy whom he liked best. This boy's name was Romeo, but everyone called him by his nickname, "Candleflame," because he was tall and thin, like a candle burning in the night.

Candleflame was the laziest, most mischievous boy in the school, yet Pinocchio felt a close friendship with him anyway. In fact, he went to Candleflame's house first of all, to invite him to breakfast, but he wasn't there. Pinocchio went back a second time, and still didn't find him. And later he tried a third time—still in vain.

Where could he have disappeared to? Pinocchio looked everywhere and finally spied him hiding under the porch in front of a farmer's cottage.

"What are you up to, Candleflame?" he asked, crawling under the porch himself.

"I'm waiting for midnight, so I can run away."

"Run away? Where?"

"Far away—as far as I can get!"

"And here I've been trying to find you all this time! I looked for you at your home three times this afternoon."

"Why? What's up?"

"Do you mean you haven't heard the news? Don't you know how lucky I'm going to be?"

"No—tell me."

"Well, starting tomorrow I won't be a puppet any more. I'll become a boy, like you and the others!"

"Huh! Good luck to you, pal."

"So tomorrow I want you to come to my house for breakfast, to celebrate!"

"But I just told you. I'm running away tonight."

"When? What time?"

"I told you—midnight!"

"And where are you going, exactly?"

"I'm going to live in a special country, the most beautiful country in the world. It's perfect there: no work, and nothing but fun!"

"And what country is that?"

"It's called Funland. Why don't you go there too?"

"Me? No, thanks!"

"Pinocchio, you're wrong! Believe me, if you come along you won't be sorry. Where else can you find a better country for us kids? No schools, no teachers, no books—nobody ever has to do homework in that heavenly land. Thursday there's no school, and every week is made up of six Thursdays and one Sunday. Listen to me—the holidays there begin on the first of January and are over the last day of December! That's the country for me, my friend! That's what I call a civilized country!"

"But what do you *do* in Funland?"

"Plenty. You spend your days playing games and having fun from morning until night. Then you go to bed, and the next morning you start all over again. How do you like that?"

"Hmm," said Pinocchio, and he nodded his head slightly, as if to say, "That certainly sounds like the life for me!"

"Well, then, will you come? Make up your mind—yes or no?"

"No, no, no—and again no! I've just promised my kind Fairy to become a good boy, and I mean to keep my promise. But the sun's going down now—it's late! I have to leave at once and get home. Goodbye, Candleflame! Have a pleasant journey."

"Why must you hurry away? Where are you going?"

"Home. My kind Fairy asked me to come back before dark."

"Wait, just a couple of minutes more."

"I'll be late!"

"Just a couple of minutes!"

"But the Fairy will scold me!"

"Let her scold away! When she's scolded you enough, she'll calm down," said sly, bad Candleflame.

"Tell me, how will you get there? Are you going all by yourself, or with other kids too?"

"By myself? No, we have a group of more than a hundred boys who are going together."

"Will you walk, or what?"

"We'll ride! There's a stagecoach that takes you all the way to the luckiest place in the world to be! It stops here at midnight."

"Oh, I wish it were midnight now! I'd give anything if it were!"

"Why's that?"

"So I could see you all leaving together in the stage-coach."

"Stay a little longer and you'll see it!"

"No, no! I have to go home."

"Oh, come on. Just a few minutes more."

"I've been here too long already. The Fairy will worry about me."

"Poor old Fairy! What's the matter? Is she scared the bats will eat you up?"

"But listen!" said Pinocchio. "Are you really sure there aren't any schools in that country?"

"Not even the shadow of a school!"

"And no teachers?"

"Not one!"

"And nobody makes you do homework?"

"Never, never, never!"

"What a pleasant country!" said Pinocchio. His mouth was watering. "What a lovely country! Of course, I've never been there, but I can tell. I can just imagine it!"

"Then why don't you come too?"

"No—it's useless to tempt me. I've promised my kind Fairy that I'm going to be good, and I don't intend to break my promise."

"All right. Goodbye, then, Pinocchio! And give my regards to all the poor kids in school, and in the high school too, when you see them on the street."

"So long, Candleflame. I hope you have a nice trip! Enjoy yourself in that happy country and think about your friends back home once in a while!"

With these words the puppet turned toward home. He took a step or two, but then stopped and turned back.

"But—are you absolutely sure that, in Funland, every week has six Thursdays and a Sunday?"

"Absolutely!"

"What a country!" said Pinocchio, almost drooling at the thought.

Then, looking as though he had made up his mind once and for all, he suddenly spoke again.

"One last goodbye, then. Have a safe journey!"

"So long, Pinocchio."

"How long now before you leave?"

"Oh, just a few hours."

"Too bad! I wish it were just an hour or so! I might be able to wait then."

"What about the Fairy?"

"Well, you see, I'm already pretty late. It's all the same by now whether I get back an hour earlier or an hour later."

"Poor Pinocchio! But won't the Fairy scold you?"

"Never mind. Let her scold away. When she's scolded me enough, she'll calm down."

Already night had fallen—a dark night. Very soon they saw a small light moving in the distance, and they heard the sound of bells jingling and the blast of a bugle—but all as faint and muffled as the hum of a mosquito.

"It's here!" shouted Candleflame, jumping to his feet.

"What is it?" whispered Pinocchio.

"The carriage! It's the carriage that's coming to take me! Speak up! Are you coming? Yes or no?"

"But is it really true," asked the puppet, "that children don't have to study at all in that country?"

"Right! Right! Right!"

"What a country! What a lovely country! What a lovely country!"

CHAPTER

At last the carriage arrived. It didn't make even the slightest noise, for its wheels had been carefully wrapped in old rags tied on with bits of rope.

Twelve pairs of donkeys were pulling it. They were all exactly the same size, but different in color.

Some were gray, others were white, others were dappled a sort of salt-and-pepper color, and still others were striped with broad streaks of yellow and blue.

But the strangest thing about them was something else. These twelve pairs—that is, these twenty-four donkeys—weren't shod like ordinary draft animals. Instead, they had white leather boots—the kind people wear—on their feet.

And who was the coachman?

Picture to yourself a little man, broader than he is tall, soft and greasy looking as a lump of butter, with a smiling little face shaped like an apple, a little mouth that was always laughing, and a quiet, caressing little voice that sounded like a cat's when it purrs affectionately at the feet of the lady it belongs to.

Boys always liked him the moment they caught sight of him. They would race and fight to get into his coach first and be taken to the country of dreams and goodies, temptingly called Funland, that perhaps you can find on the map.

The coach was already crowded with boys between the ages of eight and twelve, piled up on top of one another like sardines in a can. It was painful to be squeezed together like that, and they found it hard to breathe. But nobody groaned or said "Ouch!" Not one of them complained for a second. The cheerful thought that in a few hours they'd be in a land with no books, no schools, and no teachers made them relaxed and contented. They were too pleased to notice that they were uncomfortable, or tired, or hungry, or thirsty, or sleepy.

As soon as the carriage stopped, the little coachman gazed fondly down at Candleflame and began bowing and smiling in a friendly, coaxing way.

"Ah, my fine young lad!" he said. "Tell me, would you like to join us on our trip to the lucky country we're traveling to?"

"Yes! Yes! I certainly would!"

"My dear boy, I'm sorry to tell you there's no more room inside the carriage. As you can see, it's terribly crowded now."

"That's all right!" answered Candleflame. "If there's no place inside I can just sit across the shafts behind the donkeys."

And he jumped astride the shafts by which the donkeys were harnessed to the coach.

"And what about you, my dear boy?" said the little man to Pinocchio with a flattering smile. "What are your plans? Are you coming with us too, or will you stay behind?"

"I'm staying," said Pinocchio. "I'm going home, and I'll study hard and do everything a good boy ought to do."

"Well, I wish you luck—you'll need it!"

Then Candleflame spoke up. "Pinocchio, listen to me. Come along with us and we'll all have such a wonderful time together."

"No, no, no!"

"Yes, yes, yes!" came a chorus of four voices from inside the carriage. "Come with us and we'll all have fun!"

"Come with us and we'll all have fun!" echoed another hundred voices from inside the carriage.

"But—if I do come—what will my dear, kind Fairy say?" wailed the puppet. who had been listening with excitement and was beginning to weaken.

"Don't trouble your head! Forget sad thoughts! Just remember: We're going to a place where we'll be free to play and have a good time from morning until night!"

Pinocchio didn't answer, but he gave a sigh. Then he gave another sigh. Then, a third sigh. And finally he said, "Make room for me. I'm coming too!"

"There isn't any room," answered the little man. "But—to show you how welcome you are—I'm going to let you sit up here on the coach box, on my own seat!"

"But what about you?"

"No problem! I'll just walk along beside the carriage."

"Oh, no! I can't permit that! I'd rather jump on the back of one of these donkeys," said Pinocchio.

And that's what he did. He stepped up to the first pair of donkeys and tried to jump on the back of the one to his right. But the animal turned on him sharply, banged him hard in the stomach with its muzzle, and sent him flying upside down with his legs in the air.

You can imagine how the boys who were watching this scene jeered and laughed!

But the little man didn't laugh. He walked up to the rebellious animal with a tender look on his face, pretending he was about to give it a kiss, and then bit off half its right ear.

Meanwhile, Pinocchio got up from the ground in a rage and jumped on the poor animal's back in one quick leap. He jumped so well that the boys stopped laughing and began cheering, "Hurrah for Pinocchio!" They cheered so loud and long that he thought they'd never stop.

But all at once the donkey kicked up his hind legs and

began bucking violently. He hurled the poor puppet into the middle of the street, on top of a pile of gravel.

Again there were great peals of laugher from the watching boys. And again the little man, instead of laughing, was filled with so much tender love for that restless little donkey that he kissed it and then, very neatly, bit off half the other ear. Then he called to the puppet.

"Get up on his back again, at once! Don't be afraid. That donkey had some funny notions in his head, but I've whispered two little messages into his ears now. I hope I've made him tamer and more reasonable."

So Pinocchio hopped up on the donkey once more, and the coach began to move. Soon the donkeys were galloping along at a fast clip. But as the carriage rumbled swiftly over the cobblestones, the puppet thought he could hear a voice,

so low he could hardly make out the words, calling to him.

"Poor fool! Again you've tried to do things your own way, and very soon you'll regret it all!"

Surprised and startled, Pinocchio peered all about him to see where the voice had come from. He could see no one. Meanwhile, the donkeys galloped on, the carriage kept on rolling, the children were fast asleep inside, Candleflame was snoring away, and the little man, sitting on his coach box, hummed quietly to himself and muttered a little song between his teeth:

At night everyone sleeps
Except me—I never sleep . . .

A few minutes passed. Then Pinocchio heard the same low voice again.

"Remember this, you little dumbbell. Children who quit studying and turn their backs on their books and schools and teachers so they can do nothing but play all day long always come to a miserable end! I know everything about it—believe me! And I can tell you: A day will come when you'll be crying just the way I'm crying now! But then it will be too late."

When he heard these words, whispered ever so quietly to him, the puppet was more disturbed than ever. He jumped down from the donkey's back and took hold of its muzzle as the carriage halted.

Now, just think how he felt when he saw the donkey was crying—crying just like a little child!

"Hey, little Mr. Coachman, sir!" Pinocchio called to the driver. "Isn't this surprising? This poor donkey is crying!"

"Let him cry! He'll laugh again on the day he gets married!"

"But—I think he can talk! Did you teach him to talk?"

"No, but he worked with a company of performing dogs for three years, and he learned how to bray a few words."

"Poor beast!"

"Come, come," said the little man. "Let's not waste our time watching a donkey cry. Jump up on him again, and let's get going. It's a cold night, and we still have a long road ahead."

Pinocchio obeyed at once. The donkeys started off again. And the next morning, at dawn, they arrived safely in Funland.

This country was different from any other place in the world. All the people in it were boys. The oldest were fourteen years old, and the youngest had just turned eight. The streets rang with enough shouting and laughter and other noise to drive you out of your mind. There were crowds of children everywhere. They were playing every kind of game. Some were rolling nuts, others were throwing horseshoes or quoits, and still others were playing football. There were boys riding bicycles, and little fellows rocking on wooden horses. One bunch played blind man's buff; another ran about playing tag. Some boys, in clown costumes, were practicing being fire eaters. Some were rehearsing speeches, like actors. Some were singing. Some turned somersaults. Some amused themselves by walking on their hands, with their legs in the air. Some played hide-and-seek. Some were rolling hoops. Some strutted about dressed like generals, wearing paper helmets and shouting orders to squads of cardboard soldiers. Some boys were laughing, some were shouting, some calling to one another, some were clapping their hands, some were whistling, and some clucking like a hen that has just laid an egg. All in all, there was so much lively excitement, so much chattering back and forth, and such an infernal hubbub that you'd have had to stuff cotton in your ears to keep from going deaf. Little theaters had been set up in every open square; made of canvas tents, they were crowded with children at any time of the day. And beautiful thoughts like these had been scribbled in charcoal on all the walls of the houses:

"*Horay fer toiz!*" (instead of "Hooray for toys!")

"*No mor skoolz!*" (instead of "No more schools!")

"*Don wit Uhritmittick!*" (instead of "Down with arithmetic!")

The minute they reached the city, Pinocchio, Candleflame, and the other boys who had come with the little coachman rushed into the streets to join the happy confusion. In a few minutes, as you would expect, they were making friends with everyone. Who could be happier, who could be more contented, than they were now?

And among all the endless games and amusements in which they lost themselves, the hours, the days, the weeks passed invisibly, with the speed of lightning.

"Oh, what a wonderful life!" said Pinocchio whenever he happened to meet Candleflame on the street.

"So! Now you see I was right, don't you?" said Candleflame the first time this happened. "And to think you didn't want to come! And that you had taken it into your head to go back to your Fairy's house and waste all your time studying! But now you're free of all that nonsense—books, school! And you have me to thank! Wasn't it my advice, my arguments, that got you to decide? It's only your real friends that can help you so wonderfully!"

"It's all true, Candleflame! I'm so happy now, and it's all because of you. And can you guess what the teacher used to say to me about you, of all people? He would always say, 'Keep away from that worthless Candleflame. He's the wrong kind of person to make friends with. He's sure to get you into terrible trouble!' "

"Poor old guy!" answered Candleflame, shaking his head sorrowfully. "I know very well that the teacher didn't like me and always liked to make up lies about me. But I don't mind! I feel generous enough here in Funland to forgive anybody!"

"What a noble spirit you have!" cried Pinocchio, hugging his friend affectionately and kissing him on the forehead.

Meanwhile, five months had already passed in this marvelous cuckoo-land of playing and pretending all day long, without ever seeing a school or a book. Then suddenly, one morning, Pinocchio had, as they say, a nasty surprise when he woke up. It spoiled all his fun and filled him with misery.

CHAPTER

32

And what was that nasty surprise?

I'll tell you, my dear young readers. The surprise was that Pinocchio, as he was waking up in the morning, began to scratch his head. And when he scratched his head, he discovered—

Can you guess what he discovered?

He discovered, to his absolute amazement, that his ears had grown almost nine inches long.

You know that the puppet, from the moment he was born, had had tiny, tiny ears, so tiny they couldn't be seen with the naked eye! So you can imagine how he felt when he found out they had grown so long during the night that they felt like two huge bulrushes.

He scurried around the room, trying to find a mirror and look at himself. But he couldn't find one, and so he filled his wash basin with water and looked into that instead. What he saw was something he could never have wanted to see: his own head, decorated with a splendid pair of donkey's ears.

How ashamed and miserable and hopeless he felt!

He burst into tears, and he screamed, and he beat his head against the wall. But the more upset he became, the longer his ears grew. And they kept on growing, and soon they were very hairy as well.

There was a pretty little woodchuck who lived in the room just above Pinocchio's. When she heard the hysterical racket he was making, she came down to his room to see what was wrong. She saw how disturbed he was, and spoke to him anxiously.

"What's the matter, dear neighbor?"

"I feel sick, sweet little woodchuck—so very sick. And my sickness frightens me. Do you know how to check somebody's pulse?"

"I do know a little about it."

"Then could you please check mine? And could you take my temperature, too, and see if, perhaps, I have a fever?"

The little woodchuck raised her right forepaw and put it on Pinocchio's wrist. Then she sighed, and said, "Oh, my friend, I'm afraid I must give you some bad news."

"Tell me! Tell me!"

"You have a bad fever."

"A fever? What kind of fever is it?"

"It's donkey fever."

"I never heard of donkey fever!" cried the puppet. But he understood only too well.

"All right, then, I'll tell you about it," said the little woodchuck. "I'm afraid that in two or three hours you'll no longer be a puppet—but you won't become a boy either."

"What will I be, then?"

"In two or three hours you'll really and truly be a donkey, just like the ones you see pulling carts full of cabbages and other vegetables to the market."

"Oh, poor me! Poor me!" cried Pinocchio, grabbing his ears in both hands and pulling at them savagely, as if they were someone else's and not his own.

"My dear neighbor," said the woodchuck in a gentle, soothing voice, "there's nothing we can do—it's just your fate, from now on. Don't you see? It's the law of the world, and it makes sense after all. Lazy children, who hate schools and books and teachers and never do anything but play and waste their time, turn into little donkeys sooner or later."

"But does it really have to be like that?" asked the sobbing puppet.

"Absolutely! And there's no use crying about it now. You should have used your brains when you had the chance!"

"But it's not my fault, little woodchuck! Believe me, it was all on account of Candleflame."

"Candleflame? Who's that?"

"My friend and classmate. I wanted to go home. I wanted to be obedient. I wanted to go on studying and doing well. But Candleflame said, 'Why go to all that bother? Come along with me to Funland instead! There we won't have to study. We'll just play all day long, and we'll always be happy!' "

"But what made you listen to such a bad, silly friend?"

"Why? Because, dear little woodchuck, I'm only a wooden puppet who is senseless—and heartless, too. For if I'd had even the tiniest bit of a heart, I couldn't have left the good, kind Fairy who loves me as if she were my mama, and who has done so much for me. And right now, this instant, I wouldn't be a puppet any longer. I'd be a real boy like all the others! Oh, if I ever see that Candleflame again, he'd better watch out! I'll tell him a thing or two that will give him plenty to think about!"

And he started to run out of the room. But at the door he remembered his donkey's ears and was afraid people would see them. What do you think he did then? He found a big hat made of cotton cloth and pulled it down over his head and ears—all the way down until it even covered his nose.

Then he ran out to find Candleflame. He searched everywhere—the streets, the squares, the little theaters, every place he could think of. But he couldn't find him. He asked everyone he met, but nobody had seen him.

At last he went to the house where Candleflame lived and knocked on the door.

"Who's there?" called Candleflame from inside.

"It's me!" answered the puppet.

"Just a second, and I'll let you in!"

Half an hour later the door opened. Imagine Pinocchio's surprise when he went in and saw his friend Candleflame wearing a big cotton hat that came down over his head and even covered his nose!

When he saw the hat, Pinocchio felt a little better and thought to himself, "Can my friend be suffering from the same disease I have? Can he have donkey fever too?"

But he pretended not to notice anything, and just smiled and asked, "How are you, my dear Candleflame?"

"Wonderful! I feel like a mouse in a room full of cheese!"

"Are you telling me the truth, Candleflame?"

"What makes you think I'd lie to you?"

"Well . . . please forgive me, my friend. But I do wonder why you're wearing that cotton hat that covers your ears."

"My doctor told me to wear it, because I hurt this knee.

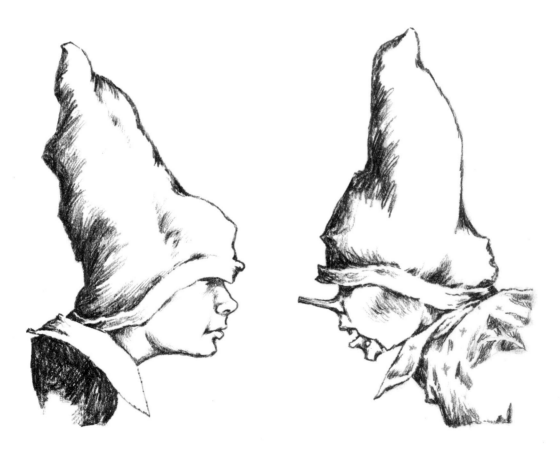

And as for you, my dear puppet, why have you pulled that cotton hat down over your nose?"

"My doctor told me to do it, because I hurt my foot."

"Oh, poor Pinocchio!"

"Oh, poor Candleflame!"

Then came a long silence, while the two friends stared mockingly at each other.

The puppet was the first to speak, in a quiet, melodious voice, very sweet and syrupy.

"I'm curious about something, my dear Candleflame. Do you ever suffer from earaches?"

"Never! And you?"

"Oh, never! Except this morning. Yes, I did wake up with an awful earache this morning."

"Me too! Exactly the same thing!"

"You too? Which ear is it?"

"Both of them! What about you?"

"Both of them. Do you think we have the same illness?"

"I'm afraid so."

"Will you please do something for me, Candleflame?"

"Sure I will! Anything!"

"May I please have a look at your ears?"

"Why not? But first let me see yours, dear Pinocchio."

"Oh, no! You first!"

"Uh-uh, dear friend. First you, then me."

"Okay," said the puppet finally. "Let's make an agreement, like good friends."

"Swell—but just what do you propose?"

"Let's both pull our hats off at the same time. Agreed?"

"With all my heart."

"Get ready!"

And Pinocchio began counting in a loud voice.

"One! Two! Three!"

At the word *three!* they both pulled off their hats and flung them into the air.

And then there was a scene you couldn't believe, except that it actually happened. When Pinocchio and Candleflame both saw, at the same time, that they had both been hit by the same bad luck, they didn't stand there feeling embarrassed and humiliated. Instead, they began wiggling their enormous ears at each other and prancing around the room, and after a while they burst out laughing.

They kept laughing and laughing and laughing until they had to hold their sides. But at the height of all their laughter, Candleflame suddenly grew quiet and turned pale and began to stagger.

"Pinocchio, help!" he cried.

"What is it?"

"Alas! I can't stand up on my two legs any more."

"I can't either," groaned Pinocchio, weeping and reeling about.

While they were saying these things, they both toppled to the floor and began running around the room on all fours. As they ran their hands became hoofs, their faces grew long and turned into muzzles, and their backs grew hairy and changed to a light gray, grizzled color, speckled with black.

But do you know what the worst moment was for these two miserable creatures? It was when they felt tails growing out behind them. That was when they felt the most disgraced, and they were so overcome with shame that all they could do was to cry and bemoan their fate.

If only they hadn't done that! For instead of crying and moaning like human beings, they brayed like donkeys. And their loud braying filled the room: *"Hee-haw! Hee-haw!"*

Instantly there came a knock at the door, and a voice from outside bellowed, "Open up! I'm the little coachman, the driver who brought you to this country! Open up at once, or you'll regret it!"

CHAPTER

T HEY COULDN'T OPEN THE
door, and so the little man
opened it himself with a good, hard kick. When he came into
the room, he gave his usual little laugh and said to Pinocchio
and Candleflame:

"Great, boys! You brayed beautifully! I recognized your
voices, and that's why I'm here."

The two donkeys stood sadly, with their heads down,
their ears sagging, and their tails between their legs.

First the little man stroked and caressed and patted
them. Then he combed them down carefully with a curry-
comb until they shone like two mirrors. Finally, he bridled
them and led them to the marketplace, where he hoped to sell
them for a good price.

There were plenty of people who wanted to buy donkeys.

Candleflame was sold to a farmer whose donkey had
died just the day before. And Pinocchio was sold to the ringmaster of a troupe of circus clowns and rope dancers. He
wanted to train the donkey to do jumping tricks and to dance
with the other performing animals.

My dear young readers, do you see now what the little coachman's real business was? That cruel little monster, who seemed to be all milk and honey, traveled around the world in his carriage. Everywhere he went, he used promises and flattery to gather up all those lazy boys who couldn't stand going to school and studying books. He would load them into his carriage and take them off to Funland, where they thought they would live forever after, playing games and making all the noise they wanted to and laughing and having fun. Then, when these poor boys turned into donkeys because all they ever did was enjoy themselves without ever learning anything, that was the time the little man had *his* fun. He would come and take them to fairs and marketplaces, and there he would sell them. And that was how, in just a few years, he had made so much money that now he was a millionaire!

I don't know everything that happened to Candleflame. But Pinocchio led a very hard life after he became a donkey, and was brutally overworked.

When he was taken to the stable after being sold, his new owner, the circus ringmaster, filled the manger with straw for him to eat. Pinocchio tried one mouthful and then spat the straw out again.

The ringmaster grumbled angrily, and then piled some hay on top of the straw. But the hay didn't please Pinocchio any better.

"Aha!" shouted the ringmaster in a rage. "So! You don't like hay either, do you? Too bad about you, my fine, choosy little donkey! I'll find a way to teach you manners, my friend!"

And with that, for a start, he lashed Pinocchio's legs with his heavy whip.

The unhappy little donkey wept and brayed with pain, and bellowed out these words:

"*Hee-haw! Hee-haw!* I can't digest straw!"

"Then eat hay!" said the master, who understood donkey language perfectly.

"*Hee-haw! Hee-haw!* I get a stomachache from hay."

"Well, well!" exclaimed the master, growing more irritated by the minute and striking him again with the whip. "Well, well! What do you want then, little gentleman? Do you propose that I feed you, a mere donkey, with broiled chicken breasts and jellied capons?"

After his second whipping, Pinocchio wisely decided to quiet down and stop complaining.

Soon his master left, locking the stable door behind him. Pinocchio remained there alone—and, because he hadn't eaten for such a very long time, he began to ache and yawn with hunger.

He yawned so hard his mouth looked like an open furnace.

At last, since he could find nothing else in the manger, he decided to try a bit of hay after all. He chewed the first mouthful thoroughly, and then closed his eyes and swallowed it down.

"Not bad!" he said to himself in surprise. "But I'd certainly be a lot better off if I'd stayed home and continued to study! Right now I could be eating a nice, fresh roll and butter, with a tasty slice of salami, instead of all this hay. Oh, well, I'll just have to be patient."

When he awoke the next morning, he went to the manger for a little more hay, but there wasn't any. He had eaten it all the night before.

So then he tried a mouthful of straw. As he chewed on

it, he had to admit the taste wasn't exactly the same as a nice dish of rice or macaroni, with or without sauce on it.

"Oh, well," he repeated as he kept on chewing the straw, "I'll just have to be patient! Anyway, I hope my misfortunes will be a warning to all naughty children who play hooky from school. Patience, Pinocchio, patience!"

"Patience, my foot!" shouted his master, who had just come back into the stable. "What do you think, my fine little donkey? Do you think I bought you just to feed you and give you water? I bought you to make you work and earn a lot of money for me. So let's get going this minute! You're going to be in the circus with me, and I'll train you to jump through hoops, and to break the paper in them with your head, and to waltz and dance the polka while standing on your hind legs!"

One way or another, poor Pinocchio had to learn all these fine tricks. It took three months, with many a blow from the whip sharp enough to skin him alive.

Finally the day came when his master felt ready to advertise a truly unusual show. Brightly-colored posters were put up on buildings at every street corner, looking like this:

That night, as you can well imagine, the theater was packed an hour before the show started.

You couldn't have found a seat anywhere, not close to the stage, not high up in the balcony, no matter how much you were willing to pay.

The seats nearest the circus ring were swarming with boys and girls of all ages. They were in such a fever of excitement that they were half crazy at the thought of seeing the famous little donkey, Pinocchio, dancing for them.

After the first act of the show, the ringmaster, dressed in a black velvet jacket, white riding breeches, and high leather boots that came up past his knees, appeared on stage. He made a very deep and fancy bow and then gave this pompous, perfectly ridiculous speech:

"Honored public, gentlemen and ladies!

"I, the humble undersigned personage, happening to be passing through this illustrious metropolitan place, desire to bring to birth for myself the honor, and the pleasure, of presenting to this intelligent and famous audience a celebrated little donkey, who has already had the respect paid to him of dancing in the presence of His Majesty the Emperor (whoever he happens to be) in the palaces of every important country in Europe and elsewhere.

"And with my very polite thanks, I graciously implore you to help us with your inspiring attendance and sympathy today and every day!"

This speech was greeted with wild laughter and much clapping. But the clapping was twice as loud, and there was a storm of applause, when the little donkey Pinocchio trotted into the center of the ring. No donkey was ever so elegant! He had a new bridle of shiny leather, with brass buckles and studs, and he wore a white camellia behind each ear. His mane was divided into tiny separate curls, each of them decorated with a colored silk ribbon. A broad girth of gold and silver went around his belly, and his tail was plaited with red and blue velvet ribbons. In short, he was the most wonderfully attractive little donkey alive.

The ringmaster went on with his speech of introduction:

"My honored listeners! I'm not standing here to tell you all kinds of lies about the great hardships I endured while capturing and subjugating this wild animal while he was still grazing freely and running from mountain to mountain on the plains of the torrid zone. Observe, I pray you, the savage fire in his eyes! All my efforts to tame him in a loving, gentle way failed, and so I've often had to rely on the friendly language of the whip! Yet all my kindness, instead of winning him over, has only made him more dangerously independent. However, following the teaching of the world-famous Dr. Gall, I've examined his skull and discovered the famous bump that the professors of medicine at the glorious University of Paris declare to be the special bump that causes hair to grow and people to do the pyrrhic dance, which you may not be familiar with. But never mind that! And because of this bump, I've been able to teach him everything—not only how to dance, but also the matter of jumping through hoops! Yes, he jumps through hoops, even when they're filled with paper inside their frames! Watch him! Wonder at him! And then judge him! Before I take leave of you, though, gracious ladies and gentlemen, allow me first to invite you to return by daylight tomorrow night for another performance. But in the apocalyptic event that rainy weather threatens, then the performance will be postponed from tomorrow night until tomorrow morning at eleven o'clock A.M. in the afternoon."

At this point the ringmaster made another very deep bow. Then he turned to Pinocchio and shouted, "Heads up, Pinocchio! Before you begin your act, kindly greet your honored audience: all these gentlemen, ladies, and children!"

At once Pinocchio knelt down obediently on his two forelegs. He remained kneeling until the ringmaster cracked his whip and shouted, "Walk!"

The little donkey rose up and began walking around the ring, keeping to a steady rhythm.

Next, the ringmaster shouted, "Trot!"—And Pinocchio, obedient to the command, changed his walk to a trot.

"Gallop!"—And Pinocchio took off at a gallop.

"Full speed!"—And Pinocchio charged ahead like a racehorse. But while he was running as fast as he could, the ringmaster raised his arm in the air and fired a pistol shot.

Pretending to be wounded, the little donkey fell down in the ring and lay there as if he were dying.

When he leapt up from the ground, there was another storm of cheering, shouting, and handclapping, and the sound seemed to reach all the way to the stars. Naturally, he raised his head and looked upward; when he did so, he noticed a beautiful lady sitting in one of the boxes. She wore a heavy gold chain around her neck. A locket hung from the gold chain, and on it was painted the picture of a puppet.

"That picture . . . it's me! That lady . . . is the Blue Fairy!" said Pinocchio to himself. He was so delighted he forgot himself and tried to call to her:

"Oh, my little Fairy. Oh, my dear little Fairy!"

Those were the words he meant to say. But instead, all that came from his throat was a hoarse braying sound. It was so loud and lasted so long that the audience, especially the children, howled with laughter.

To teach Pinocchio a lesson, and make him understand that it's bad manners to bray in public, the ringmaster rapped his nose with the handle of his whip.

The poor little donkey! He stuck out his tongue and licked his nose for at least five minutes, hoping to make it stop hurting so much.

But he felt even worse, and more desperate, when he turned to look at the Fairy again. Her box was empty; she was gone.

He felt he was going to die. His eyes filled with tears, and he could not stop weeping. But no one noticed—least of all the ringmaster, who kept cracking his whip and yelling, "Heads up, Pinocchio! Get moving! Let's show these ladies

and gentlemen how gracefully you can jump through hoops!"

Pinocchio tried two or three times. But every time he reached the hoop the ringmaster held for him, he felt more comfortable ducking under it than leaping through it. At last he did take a leap and did get through, but his right hind leg got tangled in the hoop for a second. He broke through to the other side and toppled to the ground with his body all twisted around.

When he got up again he was lame. He could hardly limp back to the stable.

"We want Pinocchio! We want the little donkey! Bring out the little donkey!" screamed all the children sitting around the ring. They were sorry for him and unhappy over his sad accident.

But the little donkey didn't appear again that evening.

In the morning a veterinarian examined him and said he'd be lame for the rest of his life.

When the ringmaster heard this, he turned to the stable boy and said, "What can I do with a lame donkey? I'd just be feeding him for nothing. Take him to the marketplace and sell him."

As soon as they got to the marketplace they found a man who wanted to buy a donkey. He asked the stable boy:

"How much for this lame donkey?"

"Four dollars."

"I'll give you one dollar. I don't need him to work for me; I just need his skin. I can see he has a nice, tough skin that will make a fine drum for our village band."

Children! How do you imagine poor Pinocchio liked hearing he was going to become a drum?

Anyway, the buyer paid the stable boy his dollar and

led the little donkey to a stony spot near the shore. Then he fastened a heavy rock around his neck and also tied a rope around one of his legs. Holding the rope in his own hand to make sure Pinocchio wouldn't escape, the man suddenly gave the animal a quick, hard shove that sent him flying into the water.

With that big rock around his neck, Pinocchio sank right to the bottom. His new owner, holding on to the rope tightly, sat down on a pile of stones to wait for him to drown so he could skin him at last.

CHAPTER

34

WHEN THE LITTLE DONKEY had been under the water for fifty minutes, his new owner said to himself:

"By now that poor little lame donkey of mine must surely be drowned. I guess I can pull him up, all right, and make my drum out of his skin."

He began hauling in the rope he had tied to one of the donkey's legs. He hauled and hauled and hauled, and at last he saw, floating on the water—can you guess? It wasn't a dead donkey floating on the water, I can tell you that! No, it was a live puppet, who was wriggling like an eel.

When he saw this wooden puppet, the poor man thought he must be dreaming. He stood there, thunderstruck, with his mouth wide open and his eyes bulging out of his head.

Then he revived a little from his first shock and, in a sad, stammering voice, asked:

"And . . . and . . . the little donkey . . . that . . . that . . . I threw into the sea . . . Where is he?"

"I'm that little donkey!" answered the puppet, laughing.

"You?"

"Me!"

"Now, come on, you little devil! Are you trying to make fun of me?"

"Make fun of you? Just the opposite, my dear master. I'm very serious!"

"But—just an hour ago you were a little donkey! And now you're a wooden puppet! How can that be?"

"It was probably the salty seawater. The sea plays funny little tricks."

"Careful there, puppet! Don't treat me like a fool! Just watch it, or I'll lose my patience!"

"Well, master, would you like to hear the whole, true

story? If you would, please untie this rope from my leg, and I'll tell it to you."

The foolish man who had bought Pinocchio when he was still a donkey was very curious to learn what had happened. He untied the knot of the rope at once. And then Pinocchio, finding himself free as a bird after such a long time, told his story.

"The first thing I should tell you is that I started out being a wooden puppet, just as I am now. And I found myself just on the edge of—almost, almost—becoming a real boy, the kind you can find anywhere in the world. But my trouble was this: I didn't like studying very much. I listened to stupid friends and ran away from home. Then, one fine day, I awoke in the morning and found that I had changed into a donkey with such long ears—and such a long tail! How ashamed I felt! It was the kind of shame, dear master, that I hope the blessed St. Anthony will never let you feel! I was taken to be sold in the donkey market, where the ringmaster of a circus bought me. He took it into his head to train me to be a great dancer and a great jumper through hoops. But one evening, during our first performance, I had a very bad fall and became lame in two legs. The ringmaster didn't know what to do with a lame donkey, and so he sent me out to be sold again, and you bought me."

"Oh, that's true, all right! And I paid a dollar for you—a whole dollar! Who's going to give me back my dollar now?"

"Do you remember why you bought me? You bought me to make a drum out of my skin! A drum!"

"Oh, yes, all too true! And now where am I to find another skin?"

"Don't give up hope, master. There are plenty of little donkeys in the world!"

"Tell me, you bad-mannered rascal, have you finished your story?"

"Not quite," answered the puppet. "Just a few more words, and I'll be through. After you bought me, you led me to this place to kill me. But then, because you felt a little sorry for me, you chose to tie a rock around my neck and to shove me into the sea. This touch of fine feeling does you great credit; I shall always remember it! On the other hand, dear master, you reckoned without the Fairy when you made your plan."

"What Fairy? Who is this Fairy?"

"She's my mama, and she's like all those other good mamas who love their children so much and are always watching over them and helping them whenever they're in trouble, even when those children, because they're so mean and so wild, deserve to be forgotten and left unprotected. Anyway, as I was about to tell you, the kind Fairy sent a great shoal of fish out to surround me when she saw I was in danger of drowning. Of course, the fish thought I was truly a dead little donkey, and so they started eating me. And what big mouthfuls they took! I would never have believed that fish could be even greedier than boys! Some ate my ears, some my muzzle, some my neck (including my mane), some my hoofs, and some the skin along my back. There was even one little fish who was so polite that he condescended to eat my tail!"

"From this moment on," said his horrified master, "I swear I'll never again put even the most delicious fish in my mouth. It would be extremely unpleasant to cut open a mullet or a fried whiting and find a donkey's tail inside."

"I agree," said the puppet, laughing, "but I have more to tell you. When the fish had eaten up all the donkey flesh on my body, they naturally started on the bones under it. Or, to be exact, they started on the *wood* under it—for, as you see, I'm made of the hardest kind of wood. After their first few bites, the greedy fish quickly learned that wood isn't meat, and that it's not made for their teeth. They were disgusted by such indigestible food and they all swam off, some one way, some another, without even thanking me. And now you know, dear master, just why it is that you've hauled in a live puppet with your rope instead of a dead donkey."

"Your story's too ridiculous!" cried the man in a rage. "I spent good money on you—a whole dollar!—and I want that money back. Do you know what I'm going to do? I'm going to take you back to the market and sell you as firewood. Good seasoned wood like you can be sold by the pound and used for kindling in a fireplace!"

"Go right ahead and sell me," said Pinocchio. "I don't mind!"

But as he said this he made one of his big frog-jumps and splashed far out in the water. Then, swimming gaily away from the shore, he sang out to his unhappy former owner:

"Goodbye, master! If you ever need somebody's skin to make yourself a drum, think of me!"

He laughed and kept on swimming. But after a while he looked back again and sang out even more loudly:

"Goodbye, master! If you ever need a bit of nice, dry, seasoned wood for the fireplace, think of me!"

In the twinkling of an eye he was so far from shore you could hardly see him. That is, all you could see was a tiny black dot whenever, from time to time, he rose from the water, leaping and doing tricks like a dolphin that's having a happy swim.

While Pinocchio was playing about in the water in this carefree way, he noticed a rock rising out of the sea. It seemed to be made of white marble, and a pretty little goat was standing on top of it. She was bleating to him sweetly, and signaling him to come nearer.

But the strangest thing was the little goat's wool. It wasn't white, or black, or streaked with both colors, like most goats' wool. No, her wool was blue—and such a blue! It was so bright and dazzling that he couldn't help thinking of the hair of the beautiful child.

Only imagine how poor Pinocchio's heart began beating with excitement! He started swimming with all his strength toward the white rock, and in a flash he was more than half-way there. But suddenly the horrible head of a sea monster

rose up in front of him. Its mouth was wide open, like a deep whirlpool, and Pinocchio saw three rows of gigantic, sharp teeth that would have scared you if you just saw them in a painting!

Can you guess who that sea monster was?

You're right! That sea monster was neither more nor less that the giant shark we've already met several times in our story. He was such a terrible killer and he had such a fearful appetite that he was nicknamed "the Attila of fish and fishermen"—after a famous king who lived long ago and murdered hundreds and thousands of people.

Think how frightened Pinocchio was now! He tried to dart away from or dodge around the monster, but that huge, gaping mouth closed in on him with the speed of an arrow.

"Hurry, Pinocchio, hurry!" bleated the pretty little goat.

And he strove desperately, with every ounce of energy in his arms and chest and legs.

"Hurry, hurry, Pinocchio! The monster is on top of you!"

And Pinocchio, gathering all his strength, swam even faster than before.

"Watch out, Pinocchio! He's right behind you! Watch out! Oh, there he is! Faster, faster, for heaven's sake! Faster! He'll get you!"

And now Pinocchio was swimming like a bullet shot out of a gun. He reached the rock, and the little goat leaned far out over the water and stretched out her front hoofs toward him to help him up.

But it was all too late! The monster caught up with him and, drawing in his breath, sucked the poor puppet into his mouth as he would have sucked an egg out of its shell. Then he swallowed him with a violent gulp that sent Pinocchio banging into the shark's stomach. The puppet landed with such a jolt that he lay there stunned for fifteen minutes.

When he recovered from the shock, he had no idea at all where he was. It was completely dark—a darkness so pitch-black that he seemed to have fallen head first into an inkwell. He listened, but there wasn't a sound. The only thing he felt, once in a while, was a great blast of wind hitting him in the face. At first he couldn't think where it came from, but then he realized it was from the monster's lungs. (I should tell you that the shark suffered badly from asthma, and that when he breathed it was like a cold north wind blowing.)

When he realized this, Pinocchio tried at first to be brave. But when the thought grew on him that he was really trapped inside the sea monster's body, he started crying and screaming and calling for help.

"Help! Help! Oh, poor me! Won't anybody come and rescue me?"

"Who do you think can come and rescue you, poor fellow?" said an unpleasant voice in the darkness, with a cracked sound like a guitar out of tune.

"What? Wh-who said that?" asked Pinocchio, frozen with fear.

"Just me. I'm a poor tuna, that's all. I was sucked in by the shark together with you. What kind of fish are you, anyway?"

"Me? I'm not any kind of fish. I'm a puppet."

"No kidding! Well, if you aren't a fish, how come you let the monster swallow you down?"

"I didn't *let* him swallow me! He decided to do that all by himself! But tell me, what are we supposed to do here in the dark, anyway?"

"We're supposed to be quiet and wait until the shark digests us!"

"But I don't want to be digested!" wailed Pinocchio, breaking into tears again.

"Neither do I!" said the tuna. "But I'm enough of a philosopher to comfort myself by thinking that, since I happened to be born a tuna, it's more dignified to die in water than in oil."

"Nonsense!" cried Pinocchio indignantly.

"Well, that's *my* opinion, anyway," answered the tuna. "And everyone's opinions, the tuna politicians say, have a right to be respected."

"Anyway, I want to get out of here!" said Pinocchio. "I want to run away."

"Run away, then—if you can find a way out!"

"Is he very big, this shark that gulped us down?" asked the puppet.

"Yes! Try to imagine—he's almost a mile long, not counting his tail!"

While they were talking, Pinocchio thought he could spy a glimmer of light far, far away.

"Do you know what that faint light is, all the way out there?" he asked.

"It must be one of our companions in misery. I suppose he's waiting to be digested, too!"

"I'm going there to find out. Do you think it might be some wise old fish who knows how we can escape?"

"With all my heart I hope so, dear puppet."

"So long, tuna."

"Goodbye, puppet—and good luck!"

"Where shall we ever meet again?"

"Who can tell? Better not even think about it."

CHAPTER

AFTER SAYING GOODBYE TO his good friend the tuna, Pinocchio began groping his way through the dark, dark tunnel inside the shark's long body. Taking first one careful step and then another—one slow step at a time—he kept moving toward the little gleam of light he had seen flickering far, far off in the distance.

As he walked, he felt himself stepping into puddles of greasy, slippery water. The puddles gave forth such a strong smell of fried fish you'd have thought it was Sunday in the middle of Lent.

The farther ahead he went, the brighter and clearer that little light shone. So he walked and walked until, at last, he reached it. And when he did reach it, what do you think he found? I'll give you a thousand guesses. He found a little table, all set for a meal, with a burning candle on it stuck in a green glass bottle. And at the table a little old man was sitting. He was so pale you'd have thought he was made of snow or whipped cream, and he was chewing on some live fish. They were so alive that, while he chewed them, they sometimes even jumped out of his mouth.

At this sight Pinocchio felt such great and unexpected joy that he almost fainted with rapture. He wanted to laugh; he wanted to cry; he wanted to say a whole world of things. But all he could do was to shout in a confused way and stammer some rambling, disconnected gibberish. Finally, though, he was able to give a cry of happiness. Tearfully, he stretched out his arms and hugged the old man and said, "Oh, my dear Papa! At last I've found you! From now on I'll never leave you again! Never, never!"

"Are my eyes deceiving me?" said the old man, wiping away tears at the same time. "Is it truly you? Is it truly my dear Pinocchio?"

"Oh, yes, it's really me! I *am* Pinocchio! And you, dear Papa—you have forgiven me, haven't you? Oh, how good you are! And to think that I, instead . . . Oh, but if you only knew all the bad luck that has rained down on my head, and how many things have gone wrong! Just think—on the day that you, my poor dear Papa, sold your jacket and bought me the ABC book to take to school, I ran away to see the other puppets. And the puppet master wanted to throw me in the fire to help roast his mutton. And then he gave me five gold coins to carry to you. And I met the Fox and the Cat, who took me to the Red Crab Inn, where they ate like wolves. And when I went out by myself, in the middle of the night, I met the murderers, who started chasing me. And I kept running, and they followed, and I ran, and they followed right behind, and I ran, until they hanged me from a branch of the Big Oak. And the beautiful blue-haired child sent a little carriage to fetch me, and the doctors came to examine me and said, 'If he's not dead, it's a sign he's still alive.' And then

I told a lie without thinking, and my nose grew so long I couldn't get through the door of my room. And that's why I went away with the Fox and the Cat to bury the four gold coins, after I'd spent one of them at the Inn. And the parrot laughed at me, and instead of two thousand coins I found nothing. And therefore, when the judge heard I'd been robbed, he sent me to prison to please the robbers. And after I was let out of prison, I saw some nice grapes in a field and was caught in a trap. And the farmer, who was right to do it, put a dog collar on me so I could guard his chicken coop. And he learned I was innocent and set me free, and the serpent with the smoking tail started to laugh and burst a blood vessel in his heart. And so I went back to the beautiful blue-haired child's house, and she was dead. And the pigeon noticed me crying and said, 'I saw your papa building a little boat to go looking for you.' And I said, 'Oh, if only I had wings like yours!' And he said, 'Would you like to go and be with your papa?' And I said, '*Would* I? But how will I get there?' And he said, 'I'll take you.' And I said, 'How?' and he said, 'Get up on my back.' And so we flew all night. And in the morning the fishermen were all looking out to sea, and they told me, 'There's a poor old man in a tiny boat who's in danger of drowning. . . .' And I recognized you right away, so far off, because my heart told me it was you, and I signaled you to come back to shore . . ."

"I recognized you, too," said Geppetto. "And, with all my heart, I wanted to come back. But I couldn't. The sea was too rough, and a huge breaker capsized my little boat. Then the horrible shark, who was close by, saw me in the water. He stuck out his great tongue and slowly, deftly, pulled me into his mouth with it and then swallowed me down like one of those bits of meat wrapped in pasta—tortellini—that the good people of Bologna love to eat."

"And how long have you been shut up inside the shark?" asked Pinocchio.

"From that awful day until now, it must be about two years. Two years, dear Pinocchio, that have felt like two centuries!"

"But how did you manage? Where did you find this candle? And matches to light it with? Who gave these things to you?"

"Wait a moment, my child, and I'll tell you all about it. First of all, the same storm that capsized my boat also sank a merchant ship. The sailors were all rescued, but the ship went down and that same shark of ours, who certainly had a hearty appetite that day, swallowed the ship just after he swallowed me."

"What? All in one mouthful?" asked the astonished puppet.

"All in one mouthful! And the only thing he spat back out was the mainmast, which got stuck between his teeth. Meanwhile, I had a great stroke of luck. The ship's larder was crammed with supplies: cans of preserved meat, boxes of biscuits and dried toast, bottles of wine, and many other things—raisins, cheese, coffee, sugar, candles, matches, and so on. With all this help from God, I've been able to get along very well for the past two years. But now, just today, it's all used up. There's no food left, and this candle that's burning away is the last one."

"What happens next?"

"What happens next. dear boy, is that we'll both be sitting here in the dark."

"Well, then, my dear Papa," said Pinocchio, "we've no time to lose. We'll have to find a way to escape right now."

"Escape? But how?"

"We'll have to go back out through the shark's mouth, and then start swimming in the sea."

"A good plan, Pinocchio! But you see, my dear, I can't swim."

"What difference does that make? You know what a good swimmer I am! I'll carry you on my shoulders, and we'll reach shore safe and sound."

"You're just dreaming, my son," replied Geppetto, shaking his white head and smiling sadly. "Do you really believe a little puppet like you, barely three feet tall, has the strength to swim in the sea with me sitting on his shoulders?"

"Let's try it, and we'll see! Besides, if it's our fate to die today, at least we'll have the great comfort of dying together."

And without another word on the matter, Pinocchio took the candle in his hand to light the way and started walking.

"Follow me," he said to Geppetto, "and don't be afraid!"

They walked and walked, all the way through the shark's body and through his stomach, too. Then, when they reached the opening of the monster's vast throat, they decided to stop and look around so that they would be ready to seize the right moment to escape.

Now, since the shark was very old, and had a weak heart, and—as you know—suffered from asthma, he had to sleep with his mouth open. So when Pinocchio peered up through the monster's throat from inside, he could see far beyond the enormous, gaping mouth—all the way up to the starry sky and the beautiful light of the full moon.

"Now is the time!" he whispered to his papa. "The shark is sleeping like a baby. The sea is calm, and it's bright as day out there tonight. Let's go, Papa! We're going to escape! Follow me, and soon we'll be free!"

And up they climbed at once through the long tunnel of that seemingly endless throat. When they reached the shark's mouth, they began tiptoeing down the tongue, which was wider and longer than any garden path in the world. At last they came to the end of it, and were ready to make the great leap into the sea and start swimming away. But just at that very moment, the shark happened to sneeze. The sneeze was so violent that it hurled Pinocchio and Geppetto all the way back down to the pit of the monster's stomach.

They fell with such a mighty bump that the candle went out, and father and son were left in total darkness.

"Oh, no! What now?" exclaimed Pinocchio anxiously.

"Now, my boy, we're simply doomed."

"Never! Why do you say that? Give me your hand, dear little Papa, and be careful not to slip."

"What are you doing?"

"We have to try all over again. Don't worry—we'll escape! Follow me and don't be afraid."

Pinocchio took Geppetto's hand and, once more, walking on tiptoe, they made their way together up the monster's throat. They then went along his tongue again, and after that they climbed over his three rows of teeth. Just before they made their great leap, Pinocchio said, "Climb up on my back, dear Papa, and hold on as tight as you can. I'll take care of the rest."

As soon as Geppetto had settled himself on his little

son's shoulders, Pinocchio, very sure of himself, jumped out into the water and started swimming. The sea was as smooth as oil, the moon shone with all its brilliance, and the shark slept on so soundly that not even cannon fire could have awakened him.

CHAPTER

36

WHILE PINOCCHIO WAS swimming quickly toward shore, he noticed that his papa, who was sitting on his shoulders with his legs dangling in the water, was shivering and shaking, as if the poor man had been attacked by a fit of malaria.

Was he shivering with cold, or was it fear? Who can tell? Perhaps it was a little of one and a little of the other. But Pinocchio, thinking it must be fear, tried to comfort him.

"Courage, Papa! In a few minutes we'll be safely on land!"

"But where is this blessed 'land'?" asked the little old man, getting more and more upset. He narrowed his eyes, as tailors do when they're threading a needle. "I've been looking all around, in every direction," he said, "and all I can see is sky and water."

"But I can see the shore clearly," said Pinocchio. "Forgive me, but I'm like a cat, dear Papa. I see even better by night than by day."

Poor Pinocchio was pretending to be cheerful. But in fact he was beginning to feel discouraged. He was getting weaker and weaker and was breathing heavily and with difficulty. The land was still far off, and he knew he couldn't go much farther.

However, he swam on—until at last he was completely out of breath and could swim no more. Then he looked up at Geppetto and, in a faint voice, said, "My dear Papa . . . help me . . . I'm dying."

The two of them, father and son, were about to drown together. But all at once they heard a voice like a guitar out of tune, and the voice shouted, "What's that? Who's dying?"

"We are! My poor papa and me!"

"That voice . . . I know it! You're Pinocchio!"

"Right! And you?"

"Don't you remember? I'm the tuna, your prison-mate inside the shark!"

"Yes, I do remember! How did you escape?"

"The same way you did! You showed me the way, and after you escaped I followed."

"Dear tuna, you've come just in time! I beg you, by the great love all tunas bear their children—please help us, or we're lost!"

"Gladly, Pinocchio, with all my heart! Now, both of you grab hold of my tail, and let me pull you. That's right! I'll have you on land in four minutes!"

As you can imagine, Geppetto and Pinocchio had accepted his invitation immediately. But then they decided it would be easier to let go of his tail and ride on his back. So they clambered up and sat down comfortably.

"Are we too heavy?" asked Pinocchio.

"Not a bit! You're lighter than a pair of seashells!" answered the tuna, who was as big and vigorous as a two-year-old calf.

When they reached land, Pinocchio jumped ashore first so he could help his papa do the same. Then he turned to the tuna and, with a voice full of deep feeling, said, "Dear friend, you've saved my papa's life! I can't ever find the right words to thank you. Permit me at least to give you a kiss, as a sign of my eternal gratitude!"

The tuna poked his mouth up out of the water, and Pinocchio, on his hands and knees, gave him a loving kiss. At this act of lively, unexpected affection the poor tuna, who wasn't used to such things, was so moved that he was afraid he'd be seen crying like a baby. He turned his head downward again and plunged deep into the water.

Meanwhile, a new day had dawned.

Pinocchio offered his arm to Geppetto, who hardly had breath enough left to stand up, and said, "Just lean on my arm a little, dear Papa, and let's go on. We'll take tiny steps, like two little ants, and when we're tired we can rest along the way."

"And where are we going?" asked Geppetto.

"We'll try to find a house or a hut where someone, out of charity, will give us a little bread and some straw to sleep on."

They hadn't taken a hundred steps before they saw the mean and ugly faces of two beggars by the roadside.

It was the Fox and the Cat! But you would hardly have

recognized them. Strange to think of it—the Cat, who had always pretended blindness, had finished up by really going blind. As for the Fox, he was now old, and his fur looked moth-eaten, and he was paralyzed on one side. He didn't even have his tail any more. This is what had happened: The wretched thief had become so poor and miserable that one day he'd sold his beautiful tail to a peddler, who wanted it for swatting flies.

"Pinocchio!" the Fox whimpered pathetically, "please show a bit of kindness to two poor, sick old creatures!"

"Creatures!" repeated the Cat.

"Old crooks, you mean!" replied the puppet. "You tricked me before, but you never can again!"

"Believe me, Pinocchio, we really are as poor and miserable as we look!"

"As we look!" said the Cat.

"Easy come, easy go!" said Pinocchio. "If you're poor, you deserve it. Remember the good old rule: 'Thou shalt not steal.' Goodbye, old crooks!"

"Have pity on us!"

"On us!"

"Goodbye, old crooks! Remember the old saying: 'The Devil drives a hard bargain.' "

"Don't abandon us!"

"Us!" repeated the Cat.

"Goodbye, old crooks! Remember the saying: 'Turn about is fair play.' "

And Pinocchio and Geppetto continued calmly on their way. Only a hundred yards further on, they came upon a pretty little thatched hut, with a roof of red bricks and tiles.

"I'm sure someone must live there," said Pinocchio. "Let's go and knock at the door."

And so they went up to the door and knocked.

"Who's there?" called a voice from within.

"A poor papa and his poor little son! We have no bread to eat and no place to sleep!" answered the puppet.

"Turn the key and the door will open," said the voice.

Pinocchio turned the key, and the door did open. They went inside and looked around, but couldn't see anybody.

"What a surprise!" cried Pinocchio. "Where can the owner be?"

"Here I am, up here!"

At once, father and son looked up toward the ceiling. And there, standing on a beam and watching them, was the Talking Cricket!

"Oh, my dear, dear little Cricket!" cried Pinocchio, bowing respectfully.

"So! Now you call me your 'dear, dear little Cricket,' do you? May I remind you of the time you tried to drive me out of your house and threw that heavy mallet at me?"

"You're right, dear little Cricket! Drive me out of this house now, if you want to. Or throw a heavy mallet at me. But please take pity on my poor old papa!"

"I shall indeed take pity on your papa, and on his little son, too! But I wanted you to remember the cruel way you acted that day. I wanted to show you how important it is to be kind whenever we have the chance. Then others will be kind to us too when we need it."

"You're right, little Cricket! You're a thousand times right! I'll never forget the lesson you've taught me. But, if I may change the subject, how do you happen to live in this lovely little cottage?"

"It was given to me just yesterday, by the most gracious

little goat I ever saw. And she had the most beautiful blue wool I've ever seen, as well!"

"That goat!" said Pinocchio. "Where is she now?"

"I don't know."

"When is she coming back?"

"She's never coming back. When she left yesterday, she was bleating sorrowfully, and she seemed to be saying, 'Poor Pinocchio! I'll never see him again. The shark must surely have eaten him up by now!'"

"Did she really say that? Then it was *she*—it was *she*— it was my own dear little Fairy!" sobbed Pinocchio as he burst into a flood of tears.

But soon he stopped crying, dried his eyes, and made a nice bed of straw for old Geppetto to lie down on. Then he turned to the Talking Cricket and said, "Tell me, dear little Cricket. Do you know where I can get a glass of milk for my poor papa?"

"You can get it three fields down from here. Giangio the gardener lives there, and he has some cows. If you go to his house, I'm sure he'll give you the milk."

Pinocchio ran straight to the house. The gardener asked, "How much milk do you need?"

"Enough to fill one glass."

"One glass of milk will cost you one penny. If you want it, first pay me the penny."

"I'm afraid I don't have any pennies," said Pinocchio, feeling terribly ashamed.

"Too bad, little puppet! If you don't have the penny for me, I don't have the milk for you."

"All right, then," said Pinocchio. And he started to leave.

"Hold on!" said Giangio. "Perhaps you and I can make an agreement. Would you be willing to turn the chain pump for me?"

"Chain pump? What's that?"

"Do you see that wooden machine over there near the cistern, with that wheel from which the buckets are hanging? *That*'s the chain pump. I use it to get water from the cistern (where rainwater collects) for the garden. Now, would you like to turn that wheel for me? It's not easy."

"I'm willing to try."

"Okay. Turn the wheel until you've drawn up a hundred bucketfuls of water, and I'll pay you a glass of milk for the job."

"Right!"

Giangio led the puppet over to the garden and showed him how to turn the chain pump. Pinocchio started working at once, and before he had drawn the hundred buckets he was soaked in sweat from head to foot. Never in his life had he worked so hard.

"Before today," said the gardener, "my little donkey did this for me. But now the poor creature is dying."

"Would you mind taking me to see him?" asked Pinocchio.

"I'd be glad to."

When Pinocchio went into the stable, he saw a fine little donkey lying in the straw, worn out with hunger and hard labor. Very troubled, Pinocchio stared hard at the donkey and muttered to himself:

"I'm sure I know him! I know that face!"

Bending down very close, he asked, in donkey language, "Who are you?"

The little donkey turned its dying eyes on him and stammered a reply in the same language:

"I . . . am . . . Candle . . . flame."

And then he closed his eyes and died.

"Alas, poor Candleflame," said Pinocchio gently. He picked up a handful of straw and wiped away a tear that was trickling down his face.

"How can you cry over a donkey that never cost you anything?" asked the gardener. "What about me? *I* paid hard cash for him!"

"I'll tell you," said Pinocchio. "He was my friend."

"Your *friend*?"

"We went to school together."

"To school!" howled Giangio, beside himself with laughter. "What? You went to school together with donkeys? I can just imagine the wonderful things you must have learned!"

The puppet felt too embarrassed to answer. So he took his glass of milk, still warm from the cow, and went back to the cottage.

From then on, for more than five months, he got up every morning at dawn and went off to turn the wheel of the chain pump, so that he could earn one glass of milk that was so good for his sick old papa. But that wasn't all he did. He learned to weave all sorts of baskets out of reeds and rushes in his spare time; and from his work he earned enough money to take care of all their expenses, although, of course, he had to be very thrifty. And among other things that he made, he built an excellent little wheelchair so he could take his papa outdoors on nice days for a breath of fresh air.

In the evenings, too, he practiced his reading and writing. For a few pennies, he had bought a huge book from which the title page and the index were missing, and he did his reading in this book. As for writing, he whittled a pen out of a twig. He didn't have any ink; and needless to say, he didn't have an inkwell, either. But he dipped his pen into a little bottle filled with a mixture of blackberry and cherry juice, and managed to write quite well anyway.

And so, because he was now so eager to do his best and to improve himself and earn his way by working, Pinocchio was able to take care of his sickly old papa fairly easily. He was also able to save a little money to buy himself some new clothes.

One morning he said to his papa: "I'm going to market today to buy a little jacket, a little cap, and a pair of shoes. When I come back home," he added, laughing, "I'll look so grand you'll mistake me for some great, wealthy lord!"

And he danced out of the house full of joy and good feeling. Then, suddenly, he heard someone calling his name. He looked around and saw a very pleasant, attractive snail creeping out of a hedge.

"Don't you recognize me?" asked the snail.

"Yes, no. I do, I don't. I'm not sure."

"Don't you remember the snail—the chambermaid in the Blue Fairy's house? Don't you remember the time I came downstairs to let you in, and you had your foot stuck in the door?"

"I do remember it all!" cried Pinocchio. "But tell me now, at once, my dear, beautiful little snail! Tell me—where did you leave my Fairy? What is she doing? Has she forgiven me? Has she forgotten me? Does she still think of me with love? Is she far away? May I please visit her?"

To all these excited, breathless questions the snail replied in her usual sleepy way: "My dear Pinocchio! The poor Fairy is lying in bed now, in the hospital!"

"In the hospital?"

"Oh, yes! Too true! She's had so many misfortunes! And now she's very, very ill and penniless. She can't afford even a mouthful of bread."

"No! Oh, how sad your story makes me! My poor little Fairy! Poor, poor little Fairy! If I had a million dollars, I'd come running to you with it. But all I have is these few dollars I was going to buy some new clothes with. Here's my money, little snail. Take it to my dear kind Fairy this instant!"

"But what about your new clothes?"

"What do I care about new clothes? I'll even sell these rags I'm wearing now if that will help her. Go, snail—hurry! Come back here in two days; I hope to have some more money for her then. Until this moment I've worked only to take care of my papa, but from now on I'll work five hours longer every day to take care of my kind mama too. Goodbye, snail! I'll expect to see you again in two days."

It was very unusual, but if you'd been there you'd have seen the snail running full speed, like a lizard on a long, hot summer afternoon.

When Pinocchio returned home, his papa asked, "What happened to your new clothes?"

"Oh, Papa, I couldn't find any that fit me right! Never mind—I'll get what I want next time."

That night, instead of sitting up until ten o'clock, Pinocchio sat up working until midnight. And instead of weaving eight baskets, he wove sixteen.

Then he went straight to bed and fell asleep. And as he slept, he saw his Fairy in a dream, beautiful and smiling. She came to him and kissed him, saying, "Bravo, Pinocchio! Because you have a kind heart, I forgive you for the naughty things you've done. Children like you, who help their sick and suffering parents as tenderly as you have done, deserve love and praise even when they haven't always been obedient and good. Keep being as good as you can, and you'll always be happy."

The dream ended and Pinocchio awoke, his eyes wide open with delight. It was early morning now.

And think how surprised he was when he found, a minute later, that he was no longer a wooden puppet. He had become a boy, like all the others, at last! And when he looked around his bed, he saw a beautiful little room, decorated simply but well, instead of the old thatched walls of the cottage. Then he jumped out of bed, and found a handsome new suit all ready for him, and a new hat, and a pair of leather boots that fit him perfectly.

Pinocchio put on his new clothes and then, naturally, put his hands in his pockets. He found a little ivory purse in one pocket, with these words inscribed on it: "The Blue Fairy returns this money to her dear Pinocchio and thanks him with pleasure for his warm heart." And when he opened the purse, he found forty brand-new glittering gold coins in it instead of the few dollars' worth of pennies he had saved up and then sent to the Fairy.

Next he ran to see his new self in the mirror, and he appeared to be someone else! He no longer saw a wooden puppet reflected in the glass, but a lively, intelligent-looking boy with chestnut-colored hair, blue eyes, and a glow of joy on his face as if he was celebrating a sacred holiday.

Among all these wonders that kept piling up on one another, Pinocchio could no longer tell whether he was actually awake or dreaming with his eyes open.

Suddenly he had a thought: "And my papa— where is he?" He rushed into the next room. Yes, Geppetto was there, just as healthy and lively and good-natured as he once had been. He had taken up his old trade of wood carving again, and was designing a beautiful, rich cornice decorated with leaves and flowers and heads of animals.

Pinocchio rushed into Geppetto's arms and kissed him. "May I ask you something, dear Papa?" he asked. "Why have all these wonderful changes come to us?"

"It's all because of you," replied Geppetto.

"Because of me?"

"Of course! When bad children become good, they change the whole life of a family and make it happy."

"And the old wooden Pinocchio—where is he hiding?"

"He's over there," answered Geppetto. And he pointed to a large puppet leaning against a chair. Its head was twisted to one side and drooping down, its arms were dangling, and its legs were so bent and crossed that it was a miracle the puppet was still upright at all.

Pinocchio stared at it a long time. After a while he said to himself, very contentedly:

"How strange I was when I used to be a puppet! And how glad I am that I've become a real little boy!"

Afterword

IN 1881 A RATHER HAPPY-GO-lucky yet busy Italian jour-nalist, Carlo Lorenzini, began writing a serialized story for an illustrated children's weekly. He had been using the name of his mother's birthplace, a Tuscan village not far from his own native Florence, as his pseudonym. Now suddenly, at the age of fifty-five, he was about to become immortal as C. Collodi, author of *The Adventures of Pinocchio: Tale of a Puppet*—the world's most famous children's book, translated into some ninety languages and reprinted in innumerable editions beginning with its first publication as a complete volume in 1883.

The first translation into English appeared in 1892, two years after Collodi's death. This British version, by Mary E. Murray, was the most available one until the somewhat Americanized text by Carol della Chiesa appeared in 1925; and there have been other translations as well over the years. In 1979 the late Rolando Anzilotti, the distinguished scholar who had established the Collodi Foundation and was its president, invited me to write a "new, idiomatically alive" translation in time for the book's centennial. As his letter put it:

The editions now on the market are either oversimplified (Disney, etc.) or heavy with outmoded diction. We are convinced that the new translation should be done by someone who has a ready and original verbal inventiveness. It seems to us that a poet is more likely to meet this need, even though *Pinocchio* is a prose work, because the book is at once the product of a tough-minded, witty adult imagination and somehow the very embodiment of a child's fantasy.

As it happened, this was something close to my heart—and had been ever since the days I had read *Pinocchio* to my own children and found myself improvising a colloquial, modern re-translation from the English text I was using, just to make the story more comprehensible and to convey a bit more of its bounce and energy. Writing the present translation has been not only a special sort of pleasure, but also a voyage of discovery. Without going into elaborate detail here, I must report that I soon discovered something more than the charming but sometimes starkly harsh, sometimes severely moralistic, and sometimes sentimental tale as I remembered it. Collodi's copious fantasy, his stylistic and fictional inventiveness, and his fine delight in yarn-spinning and unsqueamish love of the child-mind all converged in this offhand masterpiece. (There must have been marvelous storytellers in his family, from whom he absorbed the folklore so magically transmuted in *Pinocchio*.) From the brilliant Punch-and-Judy comedy of the opening chapters, in which Mr. Cherry and poor Geppetto have so much trouble with the demonically untamed bit of wood out of which Pinocchio will be carved, to the final moment, so startling and so touching, when the hero—now a real boy—stares at his inert, lifeless former puppet-self and rejoices in his metamorphosis, this is a work of genius.

It's a kind of allegory, certainly, in its waywardly appealing fashion, and it counterposes two deeply human, mutually contradictory passions: the passion to remain splendidly free of social and institutional restraints, and the passion to remake ourselves into ideally considerate and responsible beings. This is after all the great unresolved contradiction that makes every self to some degree an inwardly warring self and that makes for warring theories of education—and education was a subject that Collodi, despite what I have called his "happy-go-lucky" side, was quite seriously interested in. Pinocchio starts out as a purely free, independent, impersonal spirit, but is forced by the most painful kind of experience to accept responsibility. The change takes place partly because he sees, though only sporadically, that those he cares for are suffering because of him. (The transformation of Geppetto from a comic figure scrapping with his equally comic old pal Mr. Cherry to a grieving, put-upon "papa" is dazzlingly rapid—though possibly no more so than that of many a parent from carefree childlessness to care-fraught fatherhood or motherhood!) But mostly the change is enforced by the brutal lessons taught after the puppet becomes a donkey. Being a dutiful student, learning a decent trade, caring for aged parents: these are the world's hard lessons, absorbed through beatings, starvation, and exposure. We may be reluctant to admit it, but a century later, in our quite different world from Pinocchio's rural countryside dotted with little villages, our concern for our children's future and safety in a dangerous world is not—whatever our general attitudes—terribly unlike Geppetto's and the Blue Fairy's concern for Pinocchio.

Still, the genius of the book is largely comic and adventurous: the egg that turns cheerfully into a little chicken and flies out the window just when it was about to become an omelet, the glorious welcome given Pinocchio in the puppet theater, the Rabelaisian meal in the Red Crab Inn, the wild chases, the reunion with Geppetto inside the shark and their daring escape, the episode with the green fisherman that might well (except for its buffoonery) have come out of the *Odyssey* or some ancient Celtic legend—and these are hardly all the instances. In retrospect, the variety of kinds of personality and scenes, and of tonal effects—from boisterous farce to delicately fantastic whimsy to poignant immediacy to sheer joy—now seems amazing to me. And I haven't so far mentioned those archvillains the Cat and the Fox, who lead Pinocchio into so many scrapes and finally get their comeuppance amidst a shower of well-aimed aphorisms, or that saintly yet practical guru the Talking Cricket, who provides one of the heart-breaking moments of the book and reappears in the hilarious doctor scene and elsewhere.

In short, the book's richness is far beyond what I had remembered, simply from my childhood reading of a translation and the later experience of reading it to my children. When I sank myself into the Italian text I really discovered why its appeal has been so strong and so lasting as to survive every kind of inaccurate rendering, bowdlerizing, and omission of essential detail. The original crackles with vitality. When Pinocchio is desperately hungry we are desperately "yawning with hunger" too; and when he stubbornly ignores all his well-wishers' advice and plants his money in the Field of Miracles, we are as attuned to the pity of his self-deception and the cruelty of the fraud being practiced on him as if we were there with him. The mixture of comedy with pathos and of realistic directness with very pure imagination makes the book a great panorama for the child reader. There is so much to look at, to laugh at, to fix in visual reverie and think about! I have tried to be very true to Collodi's text: the literal details, the exact level of diction, the rhythm of phrasing and movement, the moments of high hilarity or excitement or fear or sudden insight, the lyrical moments, and the shifts of pace and feeling.

Obviously, I'm tempted to say a great deal more. *Pinocchio* goes far beyond being a curious little story about a puppet whose nose grows longer whenever he tells a lie. It stands comparison with the work of Lewis Carroll and Mark Twain. It's heartier and faster-moving than the others, but has psychological and "surrealist" resonances similar to those of *Alice in Wonderland* and a social compassion similar to that of *The Adventures of Huckleberry Finn*. In the largest sense, too, it gives its miraculous, volatile, forgetful little protagonist every opportunity to be as naughty and unruly and greedy as a child often has to be, and yet to be loved and cherished and helped until he becomes his best self of his own accord. Pinocchio may, at the end, exclaim, "How strange I was when I used to be a puppet! And how glad I am that I've become a real little boy!" But how glad the rest of us are that he *was* a puppet for all those pages, and what a twinge it gives us to read the final description of the now-abandoned puppet form! The new Pinocchio sees his former self as a strange object—"a large puppet leaning against a chair." All the intensity of the excitable being we have known is chillingly distanced by that first "a" and then by the figure's utter, unwonted lifelessness:

its head was twisted to one side and drooping down, its arms were dangling, and its legs were so bent and crossed that it was a miracle the puppet was still upright at all.

This language is a verbal pang of regret for the lost freedom of unselfconscious childhood. Lucky for us that Collodi recovered that world and brought its moods and fears and ecstasies to life again at the height of his mature powers.

Suffern, N.Y.   M.L.R.
March 1983

CARLO LORENZINI (1826–1890), who was born in Florence and lived there almost all his life, took the pen name Collodi from his mother's native Tuscan village not far away. The founder of two satirical newspapers, he was a well-known journalist and children's author. But his real star rose in 1881 when he began a very popular serial for a children's illustrated weekly, calling it simply *The Tale of a Puppet*. Two years later, published as a book with its famous present title, it established him forever as the most delightful of storytellers.

M. L. ROSENTHAL, Professor of English at New York University, is a noted critic as well as poet. His recent books include *Poetry and the Common Life, The Modern Poetic Sequence: The Genius of Modern Poetry* (with Sally M Gall), and *Poems 1964–1980.*

TROY HOWELL was born in Long Beach, California, in 1953. He studied at the Art Center School in Los Angeles, but most of his art training is self-taught. He believes that "life is our schooling and accomplishment our degree." He now lives in the Virginia countryside with his wife and young son. Among his many distinguished artistic achievements are illustrations for a new edition of Johanna Spyri's *Heidi.* "It was a great honor to be asked to illustrate this *Pinocchio*," he says, "because the philosophy of loving family relationships that is at the very heart of this great book is something my parents gave me, which I hope to pass on to my son."